The Truth Cookie

FIONA DUNBAR

Orchard Books ★ New York

An Imprint of Scholastic Inc.

For Helena,
who's just as scruffy and clever as Lulu.

And George,
who's lovely and not a bit like Torquil.

F.D.

BIG THANKS TO LEE WEATHERLY, LIZ KESSLER, SIOBHAN DOWD, AND HELEN CORNER, YOU FABULOUSLY TALENTED AND ALL-AROUND GORGEOUS PEOPLE. AND TO AIDEEN BLAIN, FOR ALL THE FUN IN HER KITCHEN. THANKS ALSO TO MY AGENT, HILARY DELAMERE, AND TO RUTH ALLTIMES AND ANN-JANINE MURTAGH OF ORCHARD BOOKS FOR ALL THEIR INVALUABLE GUIDANCE. MOST OF ALL, THANKS TO PANO, WHO LIFTED ME UP WHEN I WAS FLAT AS A PANCAKE.

LIBRARY OF CONGRESS CATALOGING-IN-PUBLICATION DATA AVAILABLE
0-439-82505-9

10 9 8 7 6 5 4 3 2 1   05 06 07 08 09

Printed in the U.S.A.
Reinforced Binding for Library Use
First Scholastic paperback edition, September 2005

Cover illustration © 2005 by Monica Lind
Text type was set in 12-point Gill Sans.
Display type was set in Dollhouse.
Book design by Marijka Kostiw

Contents

sweet nothings

Lulu Baker leaned over the banisters and heard another shriek of laughter from Varaminta. Was she ever going to go home? Not anytime soon, by the sound of it. Lulu had had no time alone with her dad all evening, and any prospect of it was fast disappearing.

Lulu sighed heavily and headed back to her room. She opened her dresser drawer and took out the tin. It was an old, round tin meant for storing cake, but Lulu used it for her Wodge of Stuff. She always turned to it in times of crisis. And if ever there had been a crisis, this was it.

As she opened the tin, the Wodge un-wodged itself all over the floor. Lulu bent down to pick up the pictures, notes, and cards. Here was the glitter monster that Mum had made for her when she was little, to scare off the other monster that lived under the bed. It had worked too. Here were Lulu's favorite photographs, like the one of Mum and Dad holding baby Lulu between them, and Lulu's most treasured of all, the lovely, laughing Mum-in-Muddy-Wellies photo. And here was the photo of Lulu on her fifth birthday, almost completely hidden by a gigantic cake shaped like a fairy-tale castle. Mum had used toilet paper tubes for the turrets. Long after every trace of pink icing was gone, Lulu had insisted on hanging on to the crumpled cardboard tubes.

As Lulu stared at the picture, a tear rolled down her cheek. Will I *ever* be that happy again? she wondered.

They'd made the cake together. Well, Mum had made it really, but she had managed to make Lulu feel as essential to the process as flour and eggs. After putting it in the oven, Mum had crouched beside the stove. "Come and have a look."

Lulu had stepped forward and peered through the glass oven door to watch as the cake puffed itself up.

"It's biggering!" Lulu had said.

Mum had laughed and put her arm around her. "That's it!" she'd replied. "That's *exactly* what it's doing; it's biggering!"

Lulu had stood and breathed in the delicious buttery aroma as the cake swelled some more. Now Lulu remembered how the light from the oven had made Mum's face look as if it glowed from within, as she had turned and whispered excitedly, "It's like *magic*, isn't it?"

There was no fairy-tale cake for Lulu's sixth birthday.

Crossing the street carrying her shopping bags on a rain-soaked day in March, Mum had been hit by a speeding motorbike. The biker had just started work that week with Eatza Pizza and was in a hurry to deliver the food while it was still hot. Lulu had not been able to eat pizza since.

Like any five-year-old, little Lulu couldn't understand that someone could just not be there anymore. And as there was no Mum to talk to, she settled for the next best thing: Mum's picture. It was a habit she still clung to seven years later, especially when Dad was away. And Dad was away or busy a lot nowadays, especially since he had won the Sweet Nothings advertising account several months ago . . . and since he had started dating Varaminta le Bone around the same time.

Dad wasn't away right now, but he might as well be. Whenever Varaminta was around, Lulu felt unwelcome. She had sensed the frostiness the first time she'd met the tall, glamorous, pencil-thin former supermodel, whose bubbly friendliness always turned to icy silence as soon as Dad's back was turned.

Lulu didn't like silences — not the empty kind, anyway. There were full silences, like the walking-in-the-woods-with-Dad-on-a-Sunday-afternoon silence, all peaceful and contented. But Varaminta's empty silences were like big black holes, threatening to suck Lulu in.

There was also the annoying presence of Varaminta's spoiled son, Torquil, who was the same age as Lulu. Lulu had hoped things would improve over time. Aileen had done her best to reassure Lulu of this. Aileen did the cooking and cleaning for Lulu and her dad, and Lulu often sought her advice. "Perhaps you all just need to get to know each other better," she'd said. But now, six months after Dad and Varaminta had first started dating, it was still the same pattern: all gushing girlfriend and warm brotherliness whenever Dad was looking, black hole when he wasn't.

And today . . . today had been the worst day yet. Lulu curled up with the Mum-in-Muddy-Wellies photo and told her all about it. . . .

★ ★ ★

A large chocolate cake rested on a crystal stand in the middle of the table. The silk tablecloth draped over the table was strewn with rose petals and silver sugared almonds. The slim, blond woman took a slice of cake and looked up, her ice-blue eyes and bloodred lips glinting in the strong lights.

Then —

"What's that light doing up there?" she screeched, throwing the slice down. "Are you trying to make me look like a witch? Urghhh!"

"Cut!" yelled the director.

The woman stormed off the set past the director, the camera operators, and the red-faced lighting man, into the gloom of the studio where Dad and Lulu sat.

Dad stood up. "Minty . . ."

Dad hadn't been dating Varaminta very long before he had hit on the idea of using the former model, author of *How to Be as Thin as Me*, in the TV commercials for his newly acquired Sweet Nothings No-Fat Desserts account. Naturally, he wanted to make sure that things were going smoothly. They weren't.

"Darling, thank goodness you're here!" pouted Varaminta, flinging her elegant arms dramatically around Dad. "Fix this mess for me, will you, Mikey-Wikey?"

"Yes, don't worry, I'll, er, have a word with them," said Dad. "Lulu's here!" he added.

Varaminta grimaced, then quickly remembered she was supposed to be delighted. "Oh, so she is," she gushed. "How super!" (Varaminta was the only person in the world who actually used the word "super.") "Has anyone seen Torquil?" she added. Torquil was also around, since school was out. Varaminta had brought him along to the studio, intent on getting him an appearance in the commercial. She'd had him hanging around the set all day.

Lulu had long since given up trying to be friends with Torquil. In fact, she and her best friend, Frenchy, had begun to refer to him as The Torment. A merciless teaser, he was also full of moneymaking scams, as Lulu and Frenchy had learned the hard way. They had once bought movie tickets from Torquil that, it turned out, had been made by him on his computer. They were completely worthless.

Lulu offered to go and look for him anyway.

"Okay, Noodle," said Dad vaguely, before setting off to sort out some fuzzy-focus lighting for Varaminta. Dad almost always called her Noodle. Torquil was quick to change this to Poodle, probably because of Lulu's unruly mass of curly blond hair. Although from the way he pronounced it — *Poo*-dle — it was clear that it wasn't just her hair that he meant to insult.

By the time Lulu returned with Torquil, a rotund

man in a suit had joined Varaminta and Dad. "But I'm the face of Sweet Nothings!" Varaminta was protesting. "It's only natural my son should be in the commercial too. Tell him, Mikey."

"Ah, and here he is," said Dad. He introduced Lulu and Torquil to the man. It was Mr. Dextrose himself, the president of Sweet Nothings.

"So how much am I getting paid?" asked Torquil.

"Um . . ." Mr. Dextrose looked at Torquil. Then he looked at Lulu. Varaminta shifted sideways slightly, hiding Lulu from Mr. Dextrose's view.

Mr. Dextrose shifted sideways slightly too and peered around Varaminta. "Hello," he said. Lulu smiled back.

Without taking his eyes off Lulu, Mr. Dextrose took hold of Dad's arm. "Mike, could I have a word with you . . . ?"

An hour later it was Lulu, not Torquil, who was on the set. Apparently Mr. Dextrose had been "inspired by her natural charm and vitality," and he was sure that "this extra spark of hers" was just what his commercials needed. Lulu was far from thrilled.

"Cake needs another touch-up!" called the director. A production assistant duly appeared, and the cake, wilting under the hot lights, got a fresh application of icing. "I, like, put extra sugar in, okay?" said the girl. "So it doesn't, like, melt so fast?"

"Good thinking," commended the director. "All right, ready? And — action!"

Lulu smiled at the camera. "Now Mum can have her cake . . ."

Varaminta held up a slice and said, ". . . and eat it too!"

"Perfect!" said the director. "It's a wrap. Okay, guys, let's dig in!"

Everyone assembled around the table except for Varaminta, who shot a private, withering look at Lulu and flounced off in the direction of the ladies' room.

Then Dad appeared at Lulu's side. "Good job, Noodle," he whispered.

Mr. Dextrose stepped forward. "Thank you all for a splendid job," he said. "I look forward to seeing the final product." There was a ripple of applause. He raised his plate. "Perk of the job: free cake! So enjoy!"

Everyone raised a slice and sank their teeth into it and —

"*BLECH!!*" they simultaneously spat out.

"Eurgh, that's disgusting!"

"Eeew, *salt!*"

Soggy globs of chocolate cake flew this way and that. They splattered into hair and onto shoes; they plopped all over the creamy white tablecloth and sizzled on the studio lights. One glob splattered onto Lulu's top.

"Oh no!" cried the assistant. "I could've, like, *sworn* it was sugar!"

On her way to the ladies' room, Lulu passed Torquil. He jeered gloatingly at her chocolatey front.

"Yeah, well, you're lucky you missed the cake," she told him.

"You kidding?" he smirked. "Luck had nothing to do with it! You should have seen your faces — excellent!" And he doubled over with laughter. So *he* had switched the salt with the sugar, Lulu realized. Ha, ha, very funny. Her face still puckering from the awful taste, Lulu walked into the ladies' room.

Varaminta paused in applying her lipstick and glanced up into the mirror. She was not smiling.

"Little bit of a disaster with the cake," ventured Lulu. Varaminta didn't answer. Lulu cleared her throat and began to rub at her top with damp paper towels. Varaminta sprayed several puffs of perfume into the air around herself, as if she were a rose needing protection from an annoying insect — this unwelcome child.

The scent cloud clenched at Lulu's throat. Coughing, she quickly dried her hands and headed for the door, but Varaminta stepped in her way. "Congratulations, Louisa," she purred sarcastically. "Nice little piece of upstaging there."

Varaminta always used Lulu's full name, though no one else did. Lulu just wasn't, nor ever had been, a Louisa. And she was definitely not a Loo-*Wheezer*, which was how Varaminta pronounced it.

"Look, I didn't even want to —" Lulu tried.

"Nonsense!" snapped Varaminta, baring her

expensively whitened teeth. "You may be the apple of Daddy's eye, but I know a rotten core when I see one. Don't play innocent with me!"

Lulu could hardly believe what she was hearing. "Huh? I *am* innocent. And what about Torquil? He put salt in the sugar bag! It made the cake taste disgusting!"

Varaminta was unmoved. "Well, if he did, who can blame him after the way he was treated? Really! But you . . . Let's get one thing straight right now," she continued in a low, menacing tone, taking Lulu's chin between two sharp red nails. "You can't fool me with your butter-wouldn't-melt-in-my-mouth act. Daddy's girl might have always gotten her way in the past, but things are going to be very different from now on. I'm the most important person in your father's life now, and don't you forget it. And I will not have you humiliate me like that again! Understand?"

★ ★ ★

"So now it's official," Lulu told the Mum-in-Muddy-Wellies photo. "She's definitely got it in for me." Another distant shriek of laughter bubbled up from

12

downstairs. Lulu felt that twisting inside again; something in the pit of her stomach had been growing bigger and harder as the weeks passed. She pictured it as a ball of rubber bands; a tight tangled knot of worry and hurt, anger and . . . well, guilt. Even today, Varaminta had managed to make her feel that if only she, Lulu, had done things differently, everything would be all right between them. That the problems were all her fault. And because she was ashamed of how silly that might sound, Lulu couldn't explain it to Frenchy, or Aileen, or anyone.

"Oh, Mum, I'm not a rotten apple, am I?" said Lulu to the Mum-in-Muddy-Wellies photo as she got ready for bed. It was Lulu's favorite because it was the most typical of Mum. Another picture showed her at a wedding, in a green dress. Lulu had thought Mum looked impossibly glamorous at the time, but now she could see that the dress didn't really fit Mum around the shoulders, the skirt was wrinkled, and Mum's hairdo was coming undone. Yet she still looked lovelier, Lulu thought, than Varaminta ever could.

"You were happier in Wellies," Lulu said out loud, before putting the photos back in the tin with the rest of the Wodge of Stuff. As she leaned down, she heard a floorboard creak. Someone was right outside her door, which was slightly ajar. Lulu crept over and yanked the door open fully, just in time to see a familiar figure disappearing down the stairs. Torquil! The last time she'd seen him, he was fast asleep on the couch; she'd forgotten all about him.

Hot Cinnamon Jelly Bean

"Here, Lulu, you gotta put your hair up, girl!" said Aileen, waving a scrunchie in her direction.

Lulu was decorating a cake, a passion she shared with her mother. She was experimenting with a Caribbean theme and had covered the entire surface of the kitchen table with shredded coconut, marzipan bananas, papaya pieces, and pictures torn from vacation brochures. She took the scrunchie from Aileen and scraped her hair into something vaguely resembling a ponytail.

"Torquil teases me about my hair. Calls me Poodle."

Aileen shrugged it off. "Oh, don't pay any attention. Worst thing you can do is let him get to you. Anyway, I think you've got gorgeous hair."

Good old Aileen; she always said the right thing. Lulu brightened.

"It'd be even lovelier if you combed it occasionally!" added Aileen. She also always spoke her mind.

Since Lulu's mum died, housekeepers and

nannies had come and gone. Most had been perfectly nice, but somehow they'd had no effect on Lulu. Aileen was different; she was a *friend*. Dad seemed happier since she was around too; she made him laugh.

For most of the two years Aileen had been with them, she had lived in . . . until the time came when they needed to make room for Varaminta and Torquil. Cheerily adapting to the situation, Aileen had rented an apartment nearby and now came over five days a week. If it bothered her, she didn't show it. Lulu, on the other hand, felt great waves of sadness whenever she remembered how much nicer it had been when it was just the three of them.

"Aileen?"

"Yeah?"

"What do you think of Varaminta?"

"Oh, she's completely fab!" said Aileen, breaking off a piece of marzipan.

Lulu turned and stared at her. "You don't mean that."

Aileen averted her eyes and began molding the marzipan vigorously. "I can't say I know her that well yet. But if your dad likes her, I'm sure she's really great." She put her head on one side as she examined her work. "That's not a very convincing banana."

"No, it isn't," said Lulu sadly.

Aileen bit her lip. "Oh, Lu, I've told you, give her time. These things are never easy, 'specially with you Poms!" she added jokingly. Aileen was from Melbourne and was always teasing Lulu about "you Poms," which is Australian for "you English people." "I mean," she went on, "it takes you people about thirty-seven years just to get around to saying 'hello' to your next-door neighbors!"

Lulu gave her a wry smile.

"Oh, she'll lighten up," Aileen assured her, "when she's more relaxed around you."

Relaxed. Lulu found it hard to imagine Varaminta relaxed. Lulu likened everyone she knew to something sweet: Dad was a chocolate éclair: shiny and businesslike on the outside (for work), but with a gooey, mushy center (for Lulu). Aileen was strawberry sherbet: bright and rosy and fizzing with energy. But Varaminta: To compare her to a mint would be to suggest there was something refreshing

17

about her iciness. She was more like a cough drop, hard-boiled and foul-tasting. As for Torquil, he was the hot cinnamon–flavored jelly bean that fooled Lulu into thinking it was cherry until it was too late, and then she'd already burned the roof of her mouth.

"Mind you," added Aileen. "I'm having a hard time getting used to that dog."

"Oh boy, me too!" said Lulu. Varaminta's doglet, Poochie, was tiny and very hairy. Lulu usually liked dogs, but this one was more like a cross between a fluffy slipper and a deranged ferret, and it seemed constantly on the edge of a nervous breakdown.

Right on cue came Poochie's yapping from outside as the doorbell rang. "WOW-WOW! WOW-wowoWOW!"

"Oh no," groaned Lulu, as she went to let them in. "They're early!" Dad had mentioned that morning that Varaminta and Torquil would be coming over. Some Sweet Nothings people were coming for dinner, and Varaminta had absolutely insisted that she should be there, "to offer my little Mikey-Wikey any support he might need." To show off your son again was more like it, thought Lulu to herself.

Lulu had hoped to get her cake project out of the way before they arrived, but no such luck. Varaminta burst in and swished past Lulu, completely ignoring her, while Torquil sauntered in and sneered behind her.

"All right, my darling. Yes, yes, yes!" said Varaminta to the dog, taking him from his designer dog carrier. "Woochie-kins WILL get his yum-yums, YES!" she went on as she followed Lulu back into the kitchen. Then she saw the kitchen table, and her voice turned from puppy slush to solid ice. "What's this mess?"

"Lulu's just decorating some cakes for a school sale, aren'tcha, Lu?" said Aileen.

"Yes, it won't take long," said Lulu quickly. "I'll clean everything up, I promise."

"You'll clean it up this instant; we have to get ready for our guests," snapped Varaminta. "This is important business, you know, not some silly —"

". . . Project for charity," Aileen interrupted. "Starving children in Africa."

Varaminta's powder-blue sandal squished into some scraps of icing that had fallen on the floor.

"Ugh! I'm going to go and freshen up; if I stay here a minute longer, my entire outfit will be ruined, and we might as well ship that off to Africa too. When I come back, there had better not be a scrap of this *orange icing* in sight!" She said "orange icing" the way most people say "dog poop." "And I suggest you clean up *your* shoes before you go anywhere else in the house, Louisa."

"No worries," Aileen reassured her. "Oh, by the way, Lulu. That reminds me, I called a repairman to come; the washing machine's making a funny noise. Sort of, 'eauw, eauw!'" she said, imitating a grinding croak. "Will you tell your dad for me when he gets in?"

"Sure." Lulu nodded. As she did, she couldn't help noticing that Torquil had grown curiously red-faced. She might have wondered more about this, had he not suddenly thrust a pack of cards under her nose.

"Hey, Poodle," he shouted, "I got those Mutant Droid cards I told you about." He waved the pack under her nose. "The Deluxe Plutonium Space Hologram Limited Edition. Only available in Japan!

Worth sixty pounds, but yours for only ten, 'cause I like you so much."

"Torquil, I'm not even interested in Space Hologram Mutant Droids," said Lulu. She wasn't falling for another one of his shameless schemes.

Torquil rolled his eyes. "*Duh!* Hello? It's an investment? It'll triple in value once the Limited Edition sells out."

"Watch it, Lulu," nudged Aileen. "The trickster's at it again."

"Torquil darling," said Varaminta, tossing her shimmering multi-tinted head of hair as she paused in the doorway, "have you noticed how jealous some people are?" She turned to Aileen. "It's what we call a First-Class Business Mind. By the time he's your age, he'll have made his first million."

"Mmm, and he won't care how he gets it!" Aileen whispered to Lulu.

"What did you say?" snapped Varaminta.

"I said, Oh yeah, you can bet on it!" Aileen smiled brightly.

"Grrrrr!" said Poochie.

21

Sushi

"What this house needs is a *feminine* touch!" said Varaminta.

"Screaming out for it, darling!" agreed her friend. Waxia Legge-Suntan was almost exactly the same shape as Varaminta, but with dark hair instead of blond and sunglasses on her head. The sunglasses were *always* on her head, which made Lulu wonder if she slept in them. Varaminta and Waxia were sitting at the dining table, up to their angular chins in sample books of glossy fabrics and wallpapers. Varaminta had decided that the Baker house needed a makeover and that she was the person to do it. Lulu had heard her wheedling her dad about it the other day, making it sound as if she'd be doing him a favor by taking care of it all. All except the cost, Lulu had thought, as she'd watched Dad writing out the check, no doubt the first of many. So now Varaminta, and therefore Torquil, too, was around even more than ever. Lulu just knew that Varaminta wasn't doing this out of the kindness of her heart; she was up to something, though Lulu couldn't quite figure out what.

"Feminine touch," indeed, she thought indignantly. "Actually, I'd call those pictures a feminine touch," Lulu remarked, pointing out some framed photographs hanging on the dining-room wall. They were fascinating close-ups of flowers, which made them look otherworldly. "They were taken by my mum."

"Ugh, *photography*!" shuddered Varaminta.

"Strictly for bathrooms and pianos only!" declared Waxia Legge-Suntan.

But Varaminta didn't seem to mind that the hallway was already crammed with dozens of twenty-year-old photographs of herself in her modeling heyday; on the contrary, she was the one who had supplied them. Varaminta with big shoulders and big hair on the cover of *Vogue* magazine; Varaminta in a bikini, for some reason, on the streets of Moscow; Varaminta draped around a famous rock star of the 1980s. Lulu was about to point this out when the doorbell rang. Varaminta jumped up excitedly. "That's the lighting man!" She disappeared into the

23

hall and a moment later was dragging the visitor into the room, waving her arms around.

". . . And in here I'm thinking crystal candle sconces . . . and a Venetian chandelier!" Varaminta gabbled on as Lulu hid behind the pile of sample books and smiled to herself.

"But —" started the visitor.

Varaminta raised a hand. "No, no, I know what you're thinking," she interrupted. "It'll clash; but the room's getting a *complete* makeover, thank goodness, so you don't have to worry."

"The theme's 'eighteenth-century palazzo'!" Waxia chimed in.

"Well, yes, that sounds lovely, but —"

"But with twenty-first-century technology!" Varaminta continued, her voice taking on a fervent pitch. "Lots of concealed spotlights — I heard this was your specialty — it can do *wonders* for the complexion!" She grabbed the man by the arm. "Now you simply *must* see what I have in mind for the *bed*room. Well, come on!"

"No! That is, uh . . . I don't think you understand!"

interrupted the visitor. He held out his hand. "I'm Ian Cakebread. I live next door."

"Oh!" A flicker of irritation registered on Varaminta's face, before she hid it with a fake smile and extended her spangly fingers to shake his hand. "Super."

"It's about my cat, Sushi. She's Siamese —"

Lulu popped her head up. "Sushi? What's wrong with her?"

"Lulu! I didn't see you there. Oh, my little Soosh is gone again! I've been up and down the streets calling for her . . . nothing. This is her," he added, handing Varaminta a copy of a poster he'd made. On it was a picture of Sushi, and at the bottom in big, bold letters, it said, REWARD £50. "Simply beautiful, isn't she?" he sighed.

Torquil appeared in the doorway. "Hello," he said. "What's up?"

"Ian's cat is missing," said Lulu.

"Oh no. Sushi!" gasped Torquil dramatically. Lulu peered at him; it was most unlike Torquil to take an interest in anything but himself.

"Hello, Torquil," said Ian Cakebread. "Yes, I'm afraid so. This is the second time it's happened," he added, turning to Varaminta. "And the second time I've offered a reward for finding her." He sighed. "Well, Torquil, I'm sure you'll do your part."

"Oh, you can bet on it," said Torquil. "You know how much I love cats. I really enjoyed playing with Sushi the other day. . . ." Torquil went all misty-eyed.

"Yes, I remember," said Ian Cakebread. "We were only just chatting about her last disappearance when you were over the other day, weren't we? Well, thank you. I'll be off . . . please, look out for her."

"'Bye," said Torquil. "I really hope you find her."

No, you don't, thought Lulu. You hope *you'll* find her and get that fifty pounds.

★ ★ ★

On Sunday afternoon, three days later, Lulu and her dad were sipping hot chocolate together in the kitchen. "I'm sorry I've only got ten minutes, Noodle," said Dad. "Everything seems to be such a rush at the moment."

26

Dad was going on another one of his business trips. Oh well, thought Lulu, at least I'll have him to myself for ten minutes. But they had been in the kitchen all of two minutes when in wafted Varaminta. "I've-got-a-surprise-for-you!" she sang. Naturally, she was addressing Dad, not Lulu. She held something behind her back.

Dad took the milk from the fridge. "Don't tell me, it's a sports car . . . no? Private jet? Anything less would be an insult." Varaminta honked like an excited goose.

All right, it wasn't that funny, thought Lulu.

"Okay, I give up," said Dad, stirring his chocolate.

"Little going-away present for my Mikey-Wikey," said Varaminta, revealing the gift with a flourish: a very handsome, very expensive-looking shirt.

"Hey, great!" said Dad, taking the cellophane-wrapped package. "How did you know that I needed this?"

"Dahling, I was there when you spilled red wine on your favorite one, remember?"

"Oh, Minty, how thoughtful! Just what I need for

27

tomorrow's presentation . . . Oh, but, love, look, it's too small; there's no way I'll get into it."

"Oh, I'm sorry. . . ." Varaminta bit her lip. "But, Mikey darling, are you sure?" She prodded his middle. "Perhaps it's time that we did something about this paunchy-waunch of yours, then?"

You set that up on purpose, thought Lulu. You just want Dad to lose weight.

Just then, a strange noise came from the hall, and seconds later, Torquil came into the kitchen carrying a beautiful Siamese cat. "Hey, look who I found. Sushi!"

"Oh, bravo!" exclaimed Varaminta, clapping her hands. "Torquil, you're a star."

"Where was she?" asked Lulu.

"Just down the street, under a bush. And guess what — the reward went up this morning; it's seventy-five pounds now!"

The cat wriggled in Torquil's arms, meowing. Poochie, who had been asleep in his basket, leaped two feet in the air. "Wow-wow-WOW!"

"Caccacacack!!" went Sushi, her tiny pink mouth wide with disgust.

"Better get it next door quick!" said Torquil, grasping Sushi firmly by the scruff of the neck and racing to the front door. Sushi dangled uncomfortably from his hand, her back paws splayed.

Some cat lover! thought Lulu.

A car horn honked outside; Dad looked at his watch. "Crikey, is that the time? Sorry, love, got to go!" He swooped Lulu into his arms and gave her a squeeze. "'Bye, Noodle." Then Lulu sat down with her hot chocolate, leaving Varaminta to see him off at the door; she wasn't hanging around for the smoochy scene, thank you very much.

Lulu hated it these days when Dad had to be away over a weekend. It used to be so much fun; he would arrange for Aileen to stay with Lulu, and they'd go swimming or to the movies, and have a lot of fun. But for the third time now, it was Varaminta and Torquil who were staying with Lulu instead. And it was looking all too much like a permanent arrangement, especially with Torquil making himself thoroughly at home in the guest room, putting up his own film posters and leaving piles of books and games in there. Dad, annoyingly, didn't seem to have a problem with this, saying the room was hardly ever used, anyway. He also said he thought the weekend arrangement would be a good opportunity for them all to get to know one another, but Lulu knew who had really given him the idea in the first place. How well she remembered the stench of Varaminta's perfume as, in front of Dad, she had clutched Lulu to her breast, saying how the poor girl needed a real mother figure around, and she'd be only too happy to sacrifice a quiet weekend at her London apartment to stay with Lulu while he was away.

"Oh no, really, I'm just fine with Aileen," Lulu had tried to insist, but to no avail. So now with no Aileen around until Monday afternoon, it would be just her, Varaminta, and Torquil in the house. Oh, joy.

Hey ho, better get back to my homework, Lulu decided, as she heard the taxi roll away. She took her mug and went into the hall, just as Varaminta and Torquil came in together. "What a hero!" Varaminta gushed. "First-Class Cat Rescuer!"

"Yep!" said Torquil, his mouth twisted into a self-satisfied smirk as he pocketed the reward. That look: Lulu had seen it before. As Varaminta went into the sitting room, Lulu stood still and stared at Torquil.

"What are you looking at?" he snapped.

Lulu was dumbstruck as a horrible realization dawned: That look marked one of Torquil's nasty little triumphs. Images flashed across her mind: Ian Cakebread and Torquil, chatting about Sushi over the garden fence only a week ago, talking about the first time she was missing and the reward Ian offered for finding her. Torquil, all over-the-top, reacting to the news of Sushi's disappearance. Torquil saying he'd found Sushi "just down the street," when Ian had inspected every last inch of their street several times over. It all fit: Torquil had found Sushi because *he'd taken her in the first place*!

"I said, what are you looking at, Poodle?"

"N-nothing," said Lulu, her cheeks burning. Proof: She needed proof.

Torquil glared at her suspiciously. "Jealous!" he said finally and bounded up the stairs.

Lulu put down her mug. Okay. Where would he have kept Sushi? Suddenly she remembered Poochie

31

growling at the cellar door the other day and Torquil dragging the crazed doglet away. Ever since, there'd been that pungent smell of air freshener . . . that was it! Torquil must have used it to put Poochie off the scent, because he was hiding Sushi in the cellar. She went to investigate.

Part of the cellar was used as a laundry room — so, no, not in there, or Aileen would have found her. A small door led to the storage part. Lulu scrabbled in the dim light among broken furniture and Christmas decorations, but could find nothing. Then, just as she was about to give up, she saw it. A pale tuft of hair, snagged on the corner of a shelf unit, near the floor. Lulu bent down to pick it up; it did look suspiciously like Siamese cat hair. But wouldn't Sushi have meowed?

Lulu thought for a moment. Sushi, being Siamese, had a meow that didn't sound like a meow at all; more like a cat trying to bark — "Eauw, eauw!" — or a dog trying to meow. Or . . . like a glitch in a washing machine. Oh boy, that was it! She remembered what Aileen had said about the noise the washing machine was making, and Torquil's reaction at the time suddenly made sense. Perhaps that noise was really Sushi! And the warmth of the washer and dryer, close on the other side of the wall, might easily have lulled her off to sleep the rest of the time. Sushi did love to sleep.

There had to be more evidence. Lulu went outside to check the trash. Sure enough, she found a black garbage bag containing one stinky cardboard box, four empty tuna cans, and right at the bottom, a murky mixture that Lulu had no desire to investigate further. She had him. Shaking with fury, Lulu marched next door right then and there and rang the doorbell. She waited. As she waited, she saw a figure appear briefly at their hall window. It was Torquil.

Bet you thought you'd get away with it, didn't you? thought Lulu, as he disappeared from view.

But a moment later he was back, this time at her bedroom window. "Hey, Poodle!" he yelled.

He was holding something; she couldn't quite tell what. "Wave good-bye-ee!" he called. She squinted, and then she saw: her tin. The Wodge of Stuff!

"Oh no!" she cried, just as Ian answered the door, cradling Sushi in his arms.

"Hello, Lulu." He beamed.

"Hi, uh, that is . . ." She glanced up at the bedroom window again. Sushi's loud purr sounded like a drum roll.

"Is anything wrong?"

Lulu turned and made her best effort to smile. "No," she said at last. "I just wanted to say . . . congratulations."

French Fry

Torquil was casually bouncing a ball against the wall in the guest room. *Thok, phut,* catch; *thok, phut,* catch.

Lulu reached out, caught the ball, and glared at him.

"Oo-oo-ooh!" Torquil smirked.

"Give them back," Lulu demanded.

Torquil hissed through his teeth, then shook his head slowly. "Sorry. No can do, I'm afraid."

"Where are they?" insisted Lulu.

"Oh, don't worry. Nothing will happen to the pictures. But no letting the *cat* out of the bag, okay?" he growled. "Can I have my ball back now, missy?" he added, switching to a teasing little-boy voice.

Lulu clenched her fist around the ball and folded her arms. "No." She knew how pathetic and hopeless this was, but she couldn't help herself.

Torquil nodded in the direction of something behind her. "You might try looking up there."

Lulu turned, and in a moment Torquil had her in a half nelson, and the ball dropped to the floor.

"Ow!" cried Lulu, rubbing her wrist. Her eyes brimmed with tears.

Torquil picked up the ball and sauntered over to the desk. "I think we understand each other," he said coolly. He patted the drawer of the desk. "Locked!" he whispered. "And only I know where the key is. Ha-ha!"

Lulu ran to her room and threw herself on the bed. Just wait till Aileen hears about this, she thought. But that would have to wait till tomorrow evening; in the meantime she couldn't wait to pour her heart out to Frenchy.

★ ★ ★

"The monster!" cried Frenchy at recess the next day. She punched her hand. "Just let me at him, the bully! He's gone too far this time."

Frenchy's real name was Amanda Fry, but everyone called her Frenchy, short for "French Fry." Her lanky build and matching long, lanky hair gave her an overall frylike appearance. She wore glasses that were always slipping down her nose, and she was

36

super-brainy, which made most people think she was also very serious, but Lulu knew better. Frenchy was the only other kid in Lulu's class living in a family of two, child and parent, although in Frenchy's case the parent was her mother. Candy-wise, Frenchy was a strawberry licorice whip: a long stream of endless fun, the kind that baffled a lot of adults.

Lulu was taken aback by her friend's show of toughness. "He's very good at karate," Lulu reminded her.

"Yeah, well . . . you'll just have to outsmart him," said Frenchy, running a stick along the chain-link fence as they walked. "I don't think he can be all that clever. Sneaky, okay, but super-smart? I wouldn't be so sure. For instance, I bet he carries that key around in his pocket." She paused, turning to Lulu. "So while he's still staying over, all you have to do is creep into his room at night, and get it."

"What, and open the desk drawer when he's sleeping right there?"

Frenchy leaned against the fence and shrugged. "You might as well try. Better than stealing it, then hanging on to the key and using it after he's gone.

He's bound to notice it's missing and then — well, it's anybody's guess how he'd get back at you for that."

Lulu leaned next to her. "Hmm . . . what choice do I have? Dad's not home for days . . . although there is always Aileen."

"What, tell on Torquil?"

"Yeah," said Lulu, kicking at the fence with her heels. "She'll put him in his place. She's good at that kind of thing."

"Hmm . . . risky," said Frenchy, peeling the bark off the stick.

"Why?"

"Look, Varaminta thinks Torquil's the cat's pajamas, right? So how's she going to react once Torky-baby goes blabbing to her about nasty old Aileen being mean to him? Which he will."

"Oh, jeez," sighed Lulu. "You're right."

"The last thing you want is to get her into trouble."

"Okay, so I'll just *have* to get the stuff back myself."

The bell rang. Frenchy threw the stick down. "Look, Lu," she added, as they slowly headed back to class, "if there's anything I can do to help you out with those two, I'm there."

★ ★ ★

Lulu lay awake in the dark. She pressed the button on her watch: 12:35. This was exactly the kind of situation Lulu would usually talk through with the Mum-in-Muddy-Wellies photo, and without the picture Lulu felt as if a part of her were missing. She got out of bed, crept to the door, and peeked out; all was quiet. She made her way along the landing to Torquil's door.

Inside the guest room, moonlight filtered through the gap in the hastily drawn curtains. Lulu glanced over at Torquil; he was asleep all right, and even his light snore had a self-satisfied ring to it. She peered around the room for his clothes. Nothing on the chair — aha! There they were: a pair of pants squatting on the floor in the middle of the room. Lulu didn't take her eyes off Torquil for a second as she crept past his bed. But hold on; was that a teddy bear on the pillow next to him? Fantastic! she thought. Ammunition at last; she stored the information away for future teasing use.

But then Lulu froze in horror. It wasn't a teddy bear: It was Poochie.

A considerably lighter sleeper than just about any creature alive, Poochie had been known to go into one of his paroxysms at the sound of a banana being peeled. Bare feet on carpet might easily have the same effect, let alone rustling around in drawers. Lulu stayed rooted to the spot as she eyed the pants on the floor, pockets gaping invitingly. If only I could just . . . no, it was too risky. She turned to leave . . . and stubbed her toe on the corner of the bed. "Ow!" she squeaked. That was all it took.

"Wow-WOW!" Immediately Poochie was awake and bouncing up and down on Torquil. "Wow-wow-WOW!"

Lulu dashed for the door. But as Torquil's bedside light went on, Poochie threw himself at her feet, and Lulu fell flat on her face. As she scrambled up, a ghostly apparition loomed before her.

"*Aaargh!*" screamed Lulu.

"What on earth . . . ?" demanded the apparition, and Lulu realized it was Varaminta . . . but Varaminta without any makeup. No lips, no eyebrows. Her eyes appeared to have shrunk, and she gleamed palely like a skeleton. Lulu was fleetingly reminded of a corny sci-fi line Dad jokingly used now and then: *It's life, Jim, but not as we know it.*

"She snuck into my room!" accused Torquil.

"Wow-wow-WOW!" echoed Poochie.

"No, I —"

The Ghost of Varaminta picked up the doglet. "Oh? What were you doing, then?"

"I . . . I must have been sleepwalking . . . really, I . . . I forgot this wasn't the guest room anymore, I —"

"Try again," scoffed Torquil.

The Ghost glared at Lulu. "May I remind you this is a school night? What makes you think Torquil, or I, want to hear the neurotic ramblings of a hysterical girl? Get out of here!"

Lulu trailed dejectedly back to her room, climbed into bed, and curled up on her side. She felt the ball of rubber bands twisting in her belly again. Now what? She couldn't risk taking the situation into her own hands again; she'd only get caught. A grim realization dawned. She would either have to forget all about her Wodge of Stuff — impossible! — or tell Dad. He would be back on Wednesday, and he was her only hope. Dad would talk to Torquil, and then Torquil would have to give the tin back.

Lulu wished she could just stay in bed until then.

Spilled Candy

"Wow, this is just for me?" said Dad, halting in the doorway as he gazed at the array of flowers and candles.

"That's right," said Aileen, as she put the finishing touches on an arrangement of lilies. "To welcome you home. You know how she likes everything to look nice!"

"She certainly does," said Dad. "Mmm. Makes quite a difference . . ."

"Dad!" cried Lulu, throwing herself into his arms.

"Hey, Noodle, how are things?"

"Oh, you know," said Lulu with a shrug.

Aileen glanced at her, then at Dad.

"What's that supposed to mean?" said Dad. Then he noticed the sadness in Lulu's face.

"She hasn't been herself since Monday, but she won't tell me what's wrong," said Aileen. "See if you can cheer her up, eh?" She gave Lulu a quick hug and picked up her bag. "Well, I'll be going."

Dad smiled at Aileen. "Thanks." Then he sat on the couch and pulled Lulu toward him.

"Noodle, what's the matter?'

Lulu felt a surge of emotion, and her voice came out all shaky. "Oh, Dad, it's just . . ." A sob forced its way in, leaving her speechless for a moment. "Torquil took my tin, you know the one with all the pictures of Mum, and the cards, and . . ."

Dad blinked at her. "Why on earth would he want pictures of your mum?"

Lulu bit her lip. She couldn't bring herself to say anything about Sushi. Who knew what Torquil might do with her Wodge of Stuff? He'd probably destroy it all in revenge. No; get it back first.

"Because he just doesn't like me?" she said lamely.

"Well, he's not getting away with that sort of thing. How dare he!"

"What's the matter?" said Varaminta, as she appeared in a slinky, skimpy dress. Lulu was constantly amazed at how many different outfits Varaminta required to get herself through the day.

She had just gotten back from picking up Dad from the airport, in her airport-picking-up outfit (orange wool jacket, black dress, cream patent-leather boots, pink and orange scarf, black sunglasses), and she had already changed into this evening outfit. In the morning she had been in her designer workout gear. Followed no doubt by a lunch-with-Waxia outfit. Varaminta dressed in clothes by designers with names like Moochie and Toochie, and Lulu often wondered why all Varaminta's clothes rhymed with her dog. Or maybe the dog rhymed with her clothes.

"Lulu says Torquil took something from her room," said Dad. "A tin, with some special things inside. Where is he?"

"Well, he's upstairs, but, Mikey darling —"

"All right, Noodle," said Dad, standing up. "Let's go and sort this out.'

"Okay," said Varaminta, as he walked on ahead. "But I think you'll find that, if anything, Louisa's the guilty one," she added, throwing a sharp look at Lulu behind Dad's back.

"Torquil?" called Dad, as he pushed open the guest bedroom door. Lulu followed, while Varaminta floated up the stairs behind.

Torquil was getting ready for their return home, apparently the model son as he folded every item with scientific precision before packing it in his bag. "Oh, hello, I hope you had a good business trip, Michael," he said politely. The phony! thought Lulu.

Dad squared his jaw and circled the room. "Okay, what did you do with Lulu's tin?"

"Excuse me?" said Torquil.

"He locked it in there, Dad!" said Lulu, pointing to the desk.

Torquil blinked. "I have no idea what she's talking about. By the way, has anyone seen my Gameboy? I definitely brought it with me, and now that I need to pack it, I can't find it."

Varaminta had appeared at the doorway by now. "Mikey, Torquil really wouldn't touch anything of Louisa's. Darling, show him what's in that drawer."

"Oh, of course!" said Torquil. He pulled the unlocked drawer open and shifted his seat back.

"Please. Take a look."

46

Lulu felt sick: The drawer was completely empty.

"Where is it, then?" she challenged. "Dad, it's gone from my room. I'll show you!" She took hold of his sleeve and dragged him along the landing. "Look, it's not here!" she protested as she went to her dresser and tugged at the drawer handle. The drawer stuck, and she yanked at it hard. Finally it came free and sent her flying across the room. Gel pens, loose CDs and their broken cases, her collection of funky pencil erasers, half-eaten bags of chips, and candy spilled across the floor.

Dad looked at the mess. He cast his eye around the room, over the books and games jumbled on top of each other on the shelves, the unmade bed, the overflowing bin. "Oh, Lulu, my love," he said, rubbing her shoulder. "Frankly, it's a wonder you can find anything in this room. Hey, hang on, what's that?" He pointed to another pile in the corner. There, poking out from under some drawing pads, was the tin.

Lulu blinked. "But . . . !"

She was about to go and open it, when Varaminta

47

squawked, "What's this doing here?" She was kneeling on the floor by the dresser and had pulled something out from underneath the spilled drawer contents. She held it up.

It was Torquil's Gameboy.

Chow!

"And then, of course, I had to admit I snuck into his room on Monday night," Lulu told Frenchy, at lunchtime. "So that was that."

"What did your dad say?" asked Frenchy, biting into her sandwich.

Lulu sat in front of her untouched lunch box. "What could he say? It was my word against Torquil's, plus Torquil had Varaminta to back him up."

Frenchy pushed up her glasses and cleared her throat. "I suppose you *didn't* borrow the Gameboy?"

"What do *you* think?" cried Lulu, wide-eyed with indignation.

Frenchy raised her hands. "Sorry! So, did Varaminta yell at you?"

Lulu groaned. "Oh no, that's the even more puke-making part. She was all morally superior and forgiving, and so was Torquil. 'Oh, it's all right, Lulu, I forgive you!'" She fluttered her eyelashes.

"Oh, ew!"

"I think Dad just decided we were being typical kids and getting on each other's nerves. But you want to know the worst part?"

"What?"

"Later, I looked inside the tin."

"Oh no! It was empty?"

"No, he's too tricky for that," said Lulu, flicking the lid up and down on her water bottle agitatedly. "Oh, sure, he put stuff back — about seventy-five percent of it. French, he's still got the ones that really matter. He cornered me later, you know. Said he'd be hanging on to them for 'security purposes,' and if I told on him again . . . He's still got my favorite Mum-in-Muddy-Wellies photo, he's got *all* the best pictures. And my favorite birthday card . . . the last one I ever got from her . . ." She felt her chin wobble.

Frenchy put an arm around her.

Lulu sighed. "I've got to get those things back somehow. And there's no point in trying to get Dad to help, I realize that now. Torquil's got *her* on his side the whole time, and she can twist anything to suit them. Honestly, Dad has no idea!"

Frenchy sat back and adjusted her glasses. "Okay, you've got to use tactics," she said. "Learn to think sneaky like Torquil. He must have found some crafty hiding place and not in his room at your place — way too obvious."

"But, French, they're probably not even in the house anymore! He and Varaminta have gone home; I bet he took them with him."

"Oh, rats!" said Frenchy. She took another bite of her sandwich and chewed thoughtfully. "Still, I don't think you can assume he definitely did," she said at last. "He's a game player, by the sound of it; for all you know, he might have deliberately put them somewhere you can find them, but has some nasty trap set up."

"French," said Lulu, grabbing her arm. "You know how you said you'd help any time I needed it? Well, I need it. Look, it's Friday tomorrow. Come over and help me do some detective work!"

★ ★ ★

But Lulu hadn't bargained for Waxia Legge-Suntan and the interior decorators. Lulu had recently learned that Waxia was Varaminta's PR agent. Lulu had thought that PR was some fancy way of saying "friend," until Dad had explained that PR stood for "Public Relations," and that this was a job. He said it was sort of like advertising.

"You mean Waxia's *advertising* Varaminta, like laundry detergent?"

Dad had laughed. "No, not exactly. More a case of reminding people about her, letting them know what she's doing."

"Reminding people" about Varaminta le Bone struck Lulu as being the most awful job anyone could have, like reminding people about their worst accident. And for some reason, reminding people about Varaminta involved helping her decorate her boyfriend's home. It was a nice, comfortable house but not comfortable enough for Varaminta's skinny bottom, which apparently needed cushioning with mountain ranges of pillows everywhere and waterfalls of silk curtains that spilled from the ceiling and splashed all over the floor. The air was already filled with the perfume of dozens of Varaminta's scented candles. This was how she marked her territory.

There was some territory she hadn't been able to get her hands on, however. She had tried to talk Lulu's dad into extending the tiny shower room adjoining the main bedroom to create a large bathroom with an elaborate scroll-top bath and adjoining dressing room, but Dad had rejected the idea. The only way to do that, he reasoned, would be to take space away from Lulu's room, and that wasn't fair to Lulu.

But Varaminta had gotten her way with a lot of things. When Lulu and Frenchy came home on Friday afternoon, the sitting room had been transformed, and the hallway and landing were full of ladders and drop cloths and men in overalls.

"Louisa, I must ask you to stay in the den out of the way," said Varaminta.

Lulu frowned. "What den?"

"The television and game room," Waxia informed her haughtily. "Downstairs. Such an underutilized space, we felt."

"The laundry room?"

"Well, it's that too," admitted Waxia.

"I don't want to watch TV down there!" Lulu complained.

"Oh?" retorted Varaminta. "It's the pantry as well; I thought you'd love to be so near to all the snacks —"

At this moment, Frenchy appeared in the doorway. Varaminta quickly put on her fake "friendly" smile. "I mean . . . er, don't worry, darling. We'll make it really super in there for you, promise! And this is . . . ?"

Frenchy stepped forward and politely offered her hand. "Frenchy," she said.

Varaminta grinned toothily. "Ah yes."

In the kitchen, Frenchy said, "I take it you didn't know the decorating was starting today?"

"No."

"What about our plan?" Frenchy whispered.

"I guess it'll have to wait," muttered Lulu. She grabbed the cookie jar and slumped into a chair. "Honestly, she acts like she owns the place and Dad's made of money! It's why he's never around, you know. He won't admit it, but it is. He has to work double-hard to pay for all this. Isn't that right, Aileen?"

Aileen held up her hands. "Hey, don't drag me into this! Anyway, how do you know your dad isn't just as eager to fix the place up? I'm sure it'll look lovely when it's finished."

"Oh, right," said Lulu, sarcastically. "Dad's *always* wanted to live inside a jewelry box!" But Frenchy shot her a look, and Lulu immediately fell silent. Aileen wouldn't get involved, and it wasn't fair to expect her to. Lulu had to remind herself that Aileen wasn't her big sister, even though she often felt like one. However special she was to Lulu, Aileen was still Dad's employee, and employees could get fired. Varaminta had started making impossible demands on Aileen whenever she was over, even though Aileen didn't work for her, and it occurred to Lulu that driving Aileen away might be part of Varaminta's plan.

Frenchy helped herself to a second cookie and leaned forward. "Varaminta's sooo thin, isn't she?" she whispered conspiratorially.

Lulu leaned forward too. "Yes, probably 'cause all she eats is tiny morsels of prime bloodred steak."

"That's it!" exclaimed Frenchy, sitting bolt upright. "She's a vampire!"

Lulu burst into giggles. "Hey, no wonder she's bleeding Dad dry!" She snuck a look at Aileen, who was trying not to smile.

"Hey, Lu," said Frenchy. "Go on a garlic diet. That'll scare her off!"

Aileen coughed. "That's . . . ahem! . . . no way to talk about your dad's girlfriend." Lulu was sure Aileen's cough was concealing a laugh, and she suddenly felt sorry for her. It couldn't be much fun having someone you can't stand bossing you around and having to pretend you like them for the boss's sake. Lulu knew Aileen was doing it to try to make the adjustment easier for Lulu too. She went over and hugged her.

"What was that for?" asked Aileen.

"Oh, nothing in particular."

Aileen gave a little smile and ruffled Lulu's hair.

"Come on, Lu," said Frenchy, finishing her snack. "Time for fun and games in the den!"

"All right," said Lulu. "But first I've got to go to the bathroom."

On her way she passed the sitting room, where she could hear Varaminta talking to Waxia. Varaminta's voice had taken on a grave urgency that Lulu had never heard in her before. "It's a flop!" she pronounced dramatically. Lulu felt her ears prick up, and she couldn't resist edging closer to the door to listen. She beckoned to Frenchy.

"Nobody's buying it," Varaminta went on desperately. "And it's only two months until the paperback comes out." Lulu realized they were discussing Varaminta's book, *How to Be as Thin as Me*.

"Right," said Waxia. "The sooner you schedule the wedding, the better. Does he even know yet?" Lulu and Frenchy exchanged wide-eyed glances.

"I'm working on it," said Varaminta.

"You'd better move fast because . . . well, I might as well tell you. You know I said we could get the wedding pictures in the gossip magazines?"

"Yes?" said Varaminta breathlessly.

"Well, it's not a done deal yet, but I think I've got . . . *Chow!* magazine interested!"

Varaminta gasped.

"I know. Not just plain old *Hot* or *Envy*, but *Chow!*

So exciting. If they cover the wedding, you could get as many as seven pages. . . ."

"Seven pages in *Chow!*" Varaminta echoed reverently.

"But," warned Waxia, "they'll only be interested if it's done right. You need celebrities, so get hold of that actress friend of yours and her famous photographer boyfriend."

"I haven't seen either of them in years. . . ."

"Doesn't matter. And spare no expense; it's got to be a designer dress, diamonds, the works. And make sure Michael sticks to that diet and you get as many rooms decorated as possible. They'll want plenty of shots of your new love nest, so the more stylish interiors you can show off, the better." Waxia's voice rose with excitement. "Your book will be a total bestseller after this, guaranteed! And who knows what else? TV deals, your own line of swimwear . . ."

"Yes, yes!" exclaimed Varaminta. "I'll put my apartment on the market as soon as possible, because, let's face it, I won't be needing it for much longer!" she said gleefully. Through the crack in the door, Lulu could see her positively bouncing on the couch and clapping her hands together. Then suddenly she stopped. "Oh, but there's the girl," she groaned. "So hopelessly unpresentable, she'll ruin all the photos. Much too . . . what's the word?"

"Homely?"

"Ooh, *homely*, yes!" From the way she pronounced it, this clearly summed up for her everything that was undesirable in a person's appearance. "No elegance at all. She's already wrecked my commercial with her lousy wholesome simpering; the last thing I want is for her to wreck this as well."

"Hmm . . . Michael's bound to want her in the wedding party, though, isn't he?" said Waxia. "I don't see how you can avoid it."

Varaminta stamped her foot. "Oh, what a complete drag. But this is so important; it could make or break my career. Right, we'll have to see what we can do about the ghastly little frump. Just wait, I'll make a Moochie mannequin out of her!"

Lulu clapped a hand to her mouth. Who *did* this

woman think she was? Frenchy put her arm around her shoulder and led her away. The words swam around in Lulu's mind: the wedding, moving in, *Chow!* magazine . . . Moochie mannequin, for goodness' sake! This was getting to be too much to bear.

Stinky Burrito

Just when Lulu was expecting Varaminta to be even more of a constant presence, Lulu discovered that the Le Bones would be away for the weekend. Yet far from enjoying this peaceful interlude, Lulu found she couldn't get Varaminta and Waxia's conversation out of her mind. Her thoughts kept returning to it as she lay on the bed, looking at her substitute picture of Mum. It was a pretty grainy one, with Mum next to a Christmas tree and parts of two other people in it by mistake, but it was all she had for now. "It's a plot!" Lulu told Grainy-Christmas-Mum. And if marrying Dad was part of some sort of master plan, then for all Lulu knew, *meeting* him might have been too. Was it just a coincidence that Varaminta was trying to promote a diet book and Dad was making commercials for low-fat foods? Or had he been targeted by Varaminta for this very reason?

By Monday night, Lulu was beginning to annoy herself. "I must stop thinking like this!" she muttered to Grainy-Christmas-Mum. Maybe it was just her overactive imagination, a twelve-year-old version of her monster under the bed. Or was it? Another image began to form in her mind. A black-and-white photo of Dad, beaming proudly from the page of a trade magazine. That was it! *This* was what was bothering her so much. It was an article about him, when he'd won the Sweet Nothings account. How long ago was that? Was it before Dad met Varaminta in December — only six months ago? Could Varaminta have seen it too?

"Psst! Noodle? You awake?" whispered Dad.

Lulu jumped. Dad and Varaminta had been having an especially lovey-dovey, intimate chat downstairs when Lulu went up to bed, feeling very alone. Well, they would be, wouldn't they? thought Lulu. Varaminta had no doubt stayed away to make Dad pine for her even more. And this meant that Lulu hadn't expected him at her door at all that evening. "Yes!" she piped up. She put down the Grainy-Christmas-Mum photo and propped herself up on her pillows.

Dad shut the door and came over to the bed

with a guilty grin on his face. He sat down, took a small package from under his jacket, and unwrapped it sheepishly. "I've been dying for this!" he said, biting into a burrito just oozing with cheese. "Don't tell, will you? Varaminta would be furious!"

"Dad! I don't want your stinky food in my room."

"Sorry, but she only just went home and I couldn't wait. Mmm, this is so good. . . ."

"Dad, I need to talk to you," said Lulu.

"Ah well, that's good, because I need to talk to you too," said Dad, his voice muffled. "Wanted to catch you before you went to sleep. D'you want some?" he offered, waving the burrito under Lulu's nose.

"No!" said Lulu, pushing it away.

Dad finished it off. "Aah, that's better!" he sighed rapturously. "She's got me on this hard-boiled egg diet; it's killing me."

"You're not even fat!"

Dad wiped his mouth with a paper napkin. "I'm not skinny, either. Anyway, I've got some exciting news and some not-so-good news."

Lulu folded her arms. "You're going to tell me you and Varaminta are getting married. So what's the exciting news?"

Dad, still working on his last mouthful, stopped chewing for a moment. "You know?"

Lulu gulped, her mouth dry. "Just a hunch. So I'm right, huh?"

Dad looked curiously at her. "Yes," he said at last, shifting his gaze as he fiddled with his napkin. "That, uh, *was* the exciting news. I was waiting till we were alone together before I told you. I asked her earlier today — we met for lunch; and I don't know, suddenly it just felt right. I kind of surprised myself, to be honest — if it had been on my mind before, I certainly would have discussed it with you. But anyway . . ." He turned and took hold of Lulu's hand. "Oh, Noodle! I know this has been a difficult adjustment for you. But Varaminta thinks you're terrific. . . ."

"No, she doesn't!" snapped Lulu. "And what's more, she doesn't love you, she's using you! She only wants to get married so she can be in *Chow!* magazine."

Dad raised his eyebrows. Then he burst out laughing. "Something tells me you've been eavesdropping!"

Lulu felt her face flush. She stared at her hands, and a tear rolled down her cheek.

"Okay," said Dad, taking a deep breath. He reached over to dab at the tear with a clean corner of his napkin. "Number one: Varaminta absolutely adores you; she's always telling me how sweet and bright you are. She wants to be your friend, and she's very hurt that you don't like her. Number two: Yes, *Chow!* might be interested in covering the wedding. But Varaminta didn't even know about that before she agreed to marry me. How could she? We only got the news early this evening." His eyes met hers in a wide-open gaze.

Lulu was too stunned to explain. Here we go again, she thought; it's my word against hers, and we all know who'll win. And something else was bugging her. "If that's the exciting news," she said quietly, "what's the not-so-good news?"

"Ah. Yes, I was getting to that. You see, Noodle, I've got to go on this trip to New York."

Lulu shrugged. "You're always going on trips," she said.

"Yes, but this one is longer, and . . . well, I have to leave tomorrow. . . ."

★ ★ ★

"Almost a whole month!" Lulu told the Grainy-Christmas-Mum photo, after Dad had left her room. "And Varaminta and Torquil staying over, *to keep me company*, the whole time, as if I need that kind of company!" The way the camera had caught her, it looked as if Mum had glowing red eyes. Lulu felt the ball of rubber bands tighten as she contemplated the twenty long days stretching out ahead of her.

"How am I going to get through it?" she said. "He won't even be here for my birthday! *She's* taking me for a surprise outing instead; 'just us girls.' Ha, she adores me, can you believe that? Some way she has of showing it." Lulu suddenly remembered how Mum used to say, *There's good in everyone*, and felt a pang of guilt. Mum didn't seem to have enemies; perhaps only people with rotten cores did. Then Lulu remembered the trade magazine article. The least I could do is check when it was published, Lulu whispered to Grainy-Christmas-Mum. But Mum just gazed back at her, eyes glowing red as if warning her of danger.

Lulu tiptoed to the door and listened. Dad was taking a shower now, so the coast was clear. Five minutes later Lulu was in Dad's study, hunting through the stacks of assorted paperwork. He was bound to have hung on to the article; the only question was, where? If there was any sort of filing system, it wasn't apparent to Lulu. She was about to give up and return to her room when she noticed a piece of glossy paper pinned to a bulletin board and half hidden by some books piled in front of it. But the word "Wins" showed clearly. Lulu moved the books: This was it, the Sweet Nothings article! She looked at the date and felt a shiver run through her. It was from last November, just one month before Varaminta had appeared on the scene.

Lulu realized that this new information didn't make things any easier. But there was now no doubt in her mind: Varaminta was using Dad as a career move and didn't love him at all. Forget Mum-in-Muddy-Wellies and the other bits and pieces, this was even more important. But to save Dad, she'd have to *prove* that Varaminta had seen the article, or something similar, and then set out to ensnare him. And Lulu hadn't a clue how she would do that.

Sludgy Fudge

"Surprise!" beamed Varaminta. It was a white, bright room, with white, tinkly music. A poster for "Slim Me" showed a woman with lots of wires attached to her. A beauty salon.

Lulu felt as if a rug had been pulled out from under her. Since last night, she had actually started to believe that Varaminta was going to make a real effort to be nice to her. Since going away at the beginning of the week, Dad had been calling regularly at six o'clock in the evening. After he'd spoken to Lulu the night before, Varaminta had taken the phone, saying she wanted to discuss the birthday plans in secret. She was clearly brimming over with enthusiasm, and Lulu had taken her excitement to mean that she genuinely wanted to make Lulu happy. And Lulu loved surprises. But now she felt like a fool.

"Is this Louisa?" asked a woman in a white coat. Her teeth were so white they glowed. Lulu scowled.

Varaminta shot Lulu a furious look, then replied, "Yes, I'm afraid so. Not easy, I know, but see what you can do. The usual for us, darling." She pulled the dog from his carrier. "And Poochie-Wooch wants pink highlights, don't you, Baby Poochkins!"

The woman with the glowing teeth steered Lulu toward a sink. Some birthday, thought Lulu. She wouldn't forget this one in a hurry. Devilish thoughts ran through her head while she was robed like an angelic choir girl; there had to be *something* she could do.

Now she was staring at the ceiling while a miniature shower needled her head. Varaminta's and Waxia's voices rose above the sloshing noises.

"Any normal girl would really love all this," Varaminta went on.

"No appreciation," agreed Waxia.

"I mean, look at her, she makes no effort at all. Is it any wonder she's called Poodle?"

"Yes, we'll have to do some serious work on her in time for your big day," said Waxia.

Not if I can help it, thought Lulu.

Luminous Teeth guided Lulu to a chair in front of a huge mirror. Looking into it, Lulu could see Varaminta and Waxia reclining half naked on couches, shower caps on their heads and blue stuff on their faces. There were those little wires again, hooking them up like two Frankenstein monsters to humming machines. "What *are* those?" asked Lulu.

"They send tiny electrical impulses to your muscles, making them contract," replied Luminous Teeth. "Tones up the muscles, making you look slimmer." It occurred to Lulu that if Varaminta got any slimmer than she already was, she might disappear altogether, like in a carnival mirror. How fantastic that would be! While the Brides of Frankenstein got their lightning bolts, Poochie was having his hair painted.

In a room in the corner, another woman with bright red hair was stirring a pot of brownish stuff, like sludgy fudge.

"What's that?" asked Lulu.

"Leg wax," explained Luminous Teeth, as she drenched Lulu's head in foul-smelling goop. "For removing hair. Is this the first time you're having it done?"

"I didn't know I was! How, exactly, is the hair removed?"

"Oh, you'll be just fine. It only hurts a *teeny tiny* bit!" She said "teeny tiny" in a little-girl-talking-to-her-dolly voice. "We just heat the wax, then spread it onto those *wild old hairy legs* and then rip — uh, *gently ease* it off — and *boom!* Beautiful, smooth, silky legs."

You're out of your mind if think you're getting that stuff anywhere near me, thought Lulu.

"And . . . *kids* have this done?" she asked out loud.

"Girls want to be beautiful too. There's nothing wrong with looking your best, Louisa."

Lulu felt as if she was going to be sick. Then she had an idea: *Wait till that wax is nice and hot.*

Lulu's now de-frizzed hair hung in tendrils at the sides of her face. Luminous Teeth positioned a huge silver octopus lamp over her head. "This is to dry you off," she said. The lamp glowed hot and red, and she walked away.

Lulu went into action. She noticed a large glass container in front of her, filled with a blue liquid and some combs, labeled Barbicide.

Perfect! she thought . . . *Now!*

Lulu slid off her seat, grabbed the container, and headed for the leg-waxing room. A white coat hovered into view. "What are you . . ."

"Sorry," said Lulu, and she emptied the blue liquid down the woman's front.

"Aaaargh!"

All hell broke loose. Lulu lunged for the pot of hot wax, unplugged it, and bolted toward the door. Poochie yapped insanely while the two blue-faced monsters desperately tugged at their wires. Luminous Teeth and Red Hair descended on Lulu.

She turned: time for weapon number two.

"Nobody move!" she yelled. "I've got hot wax, and I'm not afraid to use it!"

"Call the police!" screamed Varaminta. "Do something!"

Red Hair flapped over to the reception desk. Luminous Teeth reached gingerly for the wax pot. "Now, Louisa . . . ," she said nervously. Lulu grinned, backed out of the door, then threw the pot to the floor in the doorway and hurled herself into the crowded street, leaving Varaminta trapped inside the salon by a spreading ooze of sticky, hot, fudgy goop.

★ ★ ★

Lulu weaved through the crowds, determined to get as far away as possible. She decided to jump on the first bus that came along: At that moment, it hardly seemed to matter where she ended up. One was coming now, lumbering along the road with painful slowness, a queen bee amid her army of worker taxis. Lulu thought she would burst with impatience. She glanced back down the street. A confusion of assorted onlookers had gathered outside the salon, and Lulu glimpsed a white coat, and — oh boy, a blue face! An involuntary giggle bubbled up inside her at the ridiculous sight. A moment later, she felt a stab of panic at the sight of a blue uniform.

At last, the bus pulled up. It was destined for somewhere called Angel. My guardian angel! thought Lulu. It had to be a good omen. She leaped aboard and shot past the passengers lining up to pay their fares. She wished she'd brought her purse, but then she hadn't exactly expected to need it. She bounded up to the top deck and plunked herself into the front seat, breathless. Down in the street, the policeman was now talking to a young woman, who was pointing toward the bus. *Oh boy!* thought Lulu. The bus stood still. I should've just run, she thought. Stupid, stupid. "Come *on*!" she said aloud, in spite of herself. She didn't dare look down again, but the bus finally pulled away and she was safe. Perhaps the woman hadn't seen her get on after all.

She sighed with relief. *Oh, my guardian angel, take me somewhere heavenly!* A giggle escaped her again when she saw that the man in the next seat was reading the *Guardian* newspaper.

"Yook, Mummy. She got wet hair!" said a little girl's voice behind her.

"Mmm," said the girl's mother.

Lulu suddenly realized how conspicuous she was. Dripping hair, panting, muttering . . . good grief, people would think she was crazy! Had she actually said anything *aloud* about her guardian angel? Perhaps she really was going bananas.

"She got wet hair, Mummy," repeated the girl. "Yook, Mummy, yook!"

What will happen now? Lulu wondered. She imagined Varaminta on the phone to Dad, Dad looking desperately worried and getting on the first plane home. Next there'd be Dad saying, Why did you do it, Noodle? And she would say, I did it in protest, Dad. Because you're about to make the worst decision of your life! *And* she tried to wax my legs! Then Dad would fling his arms around her and say, Oh, my love, you're right! Varaminta, you'll have to leave now. And then Varaminta would pack her bags. . . .

Oh yeah, right, she thought. And this bus will fly.

Loud breathing by Lulu's ear made her jump. She turned to see the face of the little girl, hovering next to hers. The girl was standing on her seat and leaning on the handrail.

"Why you got wet hair?"

"Maddy!" said the mother. "Sit down!" But Maddy wouldn't sit down, so her mother leaned forward and tried to pull her away. As she did so, she peered curiously at Lulu. "Are you all right?" she asked.

"Oh yes," said Lulu, smiling brightly. Don't overdo it, she told herself, you'll only attract more attention.

"Why you got wet hair?" said the girl again, her big, pale blue eyes full of concern. Lulu was touched; it was as if little Maddy could see that something was wrong. The one person on the bus whose head wasn't full of shopping lists and news and text messages was, in her little-girl way, reaching out to Lulu.

But she was also making people notice her, which was the last thing Lulu wanted.

Lulu shrugged and smiled. "Because I just washed it," she explained simply. "Oh, look!" she added, jumping up. "It's my stop. Excuse me . . . good-bye!" She raced down the stairs and out onto the street below.

Otto Lunch

Lulu found herself in a very different part of town. The crowds of shoppers were gone and most of the buildings were offices; only an occasional pedestrian strolled by. She didn't have the slightest idea what to do next, and now that the excitement was wearing off she felt kind of silly. It had been very satisfying to run away, but she couldn't escape the feeling that at some point she would have to turn herself in at the nearest police station, lost. And then it would be back to The Varmint and The Torment, and the knot of rubber bands that just kept growing inside her.

She felt her stomach grumble and remembered that she hadn't had any lunch, but there wasn't a whole lot she could do about that, with no money. A man walked by; he stared at her as he passed. Lulu peered intently into the window of a pub to avoid eye contact, and then rounded a corner into a cobbled street, trying to look as if she knew exactly where she was going. But a little way down, a most peculiar shop caught her attention.

The peeling window frame showed an old-fashioned display of ancient books. Two huge eyes stared out at Lulu from between them, and she jumped, then sighed with relief when she saw they were attached to a large, dusty, stuffed owl. Some of the books lay open, showing illustrations of antelopes and lilies and churches. Beautiful, exotic foreign dolls stood here and there, like lost characters spilled from a story long ago.

Then Lulu spotted a large bowl of fruit-colored candies near the entrance inside the shop. They looked delicious. Her mouth watered; she moved to the shop door, and squinted at a faded, handwritten sign on it. "Out . . . to . . . Lunch. Back in . . . 5 . . . mins," she read. Strange; she thought she saw someone moving around in there. Lulu pressed her face up against the glass door, which suddenly vibrated and made her nose twitch. *Zzzzzzzzzzt!* Lulu leaped. Had she pressed some alarm, or something? *Zzzzzzzzzzt!* it went again, and now she noticed another tiny sign on the door.

> Push when
>
> buzzer sounds

Lulu pushed; the door clicked open. After the bright sunshine, it was like entering a tunnel, and she paused to let her eyes adjust.

"Good afternoon!" said a man's voice.

"G-good afternoon," said Lulu, although she could see nobody. Gradually, she made out the books — lots of them, floor to ceiling — and jumped when the face of an old man appeared in the gap between some of the books. "Oh, uh . . . hi!" she said. The man came around from behind the shelves and ambled over to a large, cluttered desk. He was tiny, and rather tortoise-ish, Lulu thought, with his rounded back, shiny head, and stringy neck sticking out from the frayed collar of his shirt. He wore thick, round glasses, which magnified his eyes. He sat down and beamed at her, but said nothing.

Lulu tugged at the sleeves of her cardigan. "Umm . . . it says you're out," she said.

"Otto!" he announced.

"I'm sorry . . . ?"

"Otto Lunch, that's me," and he pointed to another sign on his desk. This one was printed. It read:

```
OTTO LUNCH
BOCKIN SMINS
```

"Most people call me Mister O," he added.

"What's 'Bockin Smins'?" asked Lulu.

"Who."

"Who?"

"Bockin Smins. Mr. Smins is my partner. He's not here today, though!" he uttered cheerfully.

"But it looks like the sign on the door says you're out to lunch and will be back in five minutes."

"Does it?" Mister O knitted his brow. "How extraordinary."

Lulu didn't know what to say to this, so she said, "Can I have a piece of candy?"

"Of course, of course, help yourself!"

"Thank you." Lulu took one and gazed around.

The shop had the aroma of Grandma's guest bedroom, mixed with a sort of two-week-old-sandwich-in-a-backpack smell. As well as the stuffed owl, there were other stuffed creatures: a fox, a puffin, and a pelican. And books, books, books. Books along the walls and books forming great towers here and there on the floor, threatening to topple over at any moment. In the middle of the room stood a table where more piles of books had grown together into a gigantic pyramid.

"How does anyone find a book in here?" she asked, helping herself to another candy. The first one had been delicious.

"Ha-ha, very amusing!" chuckled Mister O.

Lulu stopped sucking and frowned. Mister O said, "Oh, you're serious? Well, I'm proud to say that no one has ever *found* a book in this shop. If you want to *find* a book, you'd best go somewhere else. Good day!"

Lulu gave an exasperated sigh. "I didn't say *I* wanted to find a book, I only meant . . . Oh, never mind," and she turned to leave. As she did, she brushed against a tower of books and they came tumbling down, sending up a cloud of dust and knocking over the stuffed puffin. "Oh! I'm sorry!" she gasped.

"You won't be," remarked Mister O cheerfully. He didn't budge from where he was sitting, his feet up on the desk. Lulu coughed in the dust as she replaced the bird on its stand and fumbled around with the books, trying to restore some sort of order. She stacked them up, only to have them come crashing to her feet again.

Still Mister O didn't move. He just sat there, with an irritating smile.

"Can't you see I need some help?" she growled at him. "What kind of shop is this, any —"

Suddenly she stopped dead. Something had caught her eye. The book in her hand was open to the first page. On it, in faded handwriting, were the words:

For my lovely Lulu.
Happy Birthday!
Lots of love,

Mum

"OH!" she cried, and clapped her hand over her mouth. For a moment she didn't move. She just read the words over and over.

"It's found you, then!" said Mister O, as jovial as ever.

"It's — what?"

"As I said before. People don't find books in this shop. Books find people. *It* found *you*." The words went around in Lulu's head as she stared at the book: *found you . . . found you . . .*

"FOUND YOU!" screeched a voice outside the door. "That's her, officer, in there!"

"Oh no!" gasped Lulu. "Varaminta!"

The Apple Star

Varaminta cooed like a dove over Lulu, in front of the policeman. But as soon as they got home, she became a screeching harpy. "You lousy, ungrateful child! After all the trouble I went to!" Her talons dug into Lulu's arm.

"Ow! I never wanted to go to that awful place," Lulu retorted.

Varaminta's face twitched. "How dare you. You loathsome, scheming brat!" Poochie joined in, yapping and bouncing like an insane pink toy.

"Hey, what on earth is going on?" came a voice from behind them. It was Aileen.

"What are you doing here? It's Saturday," squawked Varaminta, hopping sideways and almost twisting her ankle.

"I came to make dinner, like you asked, remember? And I picked up Torquil from his friend's house at five, like you said."

Varaminta blinked at her watch. "Oh . . . yes,

right. . . . Well, things didn't exactly go according to plan today," she spat, glaring at Lulu.

Aileen moved toward Lulu and put her arm around her. "What happened, love?"

"I don't actually think it's any of your business!" snapped Varaminta.

"Oh, don't you, now?" challenged Aileen, her face flushed with anger. "Have you considered Lulu's opinion on that matter?"

"I can't talk about it," said Lulu, "but I'm fine, *really*. . . ." She turned on her heel and dashed upstairs. She didn't want to say anything that would make things worse between Aileen and Varaminta.

And they were bad enough already; behind her, she could hear Varaminta hissing at Aileen, "You should learn to keep your interfering nose out of things!"

Torquil was sitting on the banister outside Lulu's room, smirking. She walked purposefully past him and slammed her door.

★ ★ ★

Lulu didn't dare examine the book until after Torquil had gone to bed. She went to bed herself and even turned off her light. When she was sure it was safe she crept over to the dresser, where she had hurriedly shoved the little book in her sock drawer. It was a hardcover but quite small, not much more than half an inch thick. It was just as well, because it meant that she had been able to hide it under her cardigan, wedged in the waistband of her pants. As it turned out, Mister O had been wonderful; he had made sure she was ready before buzzing in the unwelcome guests. And he had insisted that Lulu should have the book, even though she couldn't pay for it. "Oh, thank you!" Lulu had gushed. As the hammering on the door increased, she gripped his sleeve. "But I'm scared!"

"Don't worry," Mister O had said kindly. And he leaned closer. "They'll get their just desserts, believe me. Happy birthday!"

Lulu had gaped at him in wonder as he buzzed them into the shop. How did he know so much about her?

Lulu wriggled farther down the bed. She was feeling almost faint with anticipation. Just what kind of book was it that had "found her" — and why? She glanced over at the Grainy-Christmas-Mum photo, propped up on the bedside table. Could the book *really* have been sent from her? Switching on her flashlight, Lulu studied the worn yellow cover. It had a small gold star on it, and in gold letters, it said:

The Apple Star
by
Ambrosia May

Strange title! she thought, and flipped through it. The disappointment she felt on discovering it was a cookbook, of all things, was almost more than she could bear. What on earth was he talking about, that crazy old man, she thought. "Books find people!" Why on earth would a cookbook be any good to me? Her stomach growled, as if agreeing with her. She turned back to the first page, with its mysterious inscription. There just had to be some special meaning to this book. Perhaps the introduction would make things clearer. She started to read.

Cut an apple in half across its width. There, in each half, you will see a five-pointed star. Two stars: One represents Venus, the evening star, also known as Hesperus; the other is your star, the one that speaks to you, and only you, across time and space. Now imagine a magnificent garden surrounded by waters. It shares its name with Hesperus, which shines above it. In this garden are three nymphs, who guard a tree that bears golden apples. Very few people ever reach into that world and learn its secrets. You are one of them.

The first secret is this: Anything and everything is possible.

The rest of the secrets that have been entrusted to me, I share with you in the following pages. Let your star guide you in using them.

Lulu suddenly noticed she hadn't breathed for several seconds, and now a puff escaped her. Goose bumps spread up her arms and her head tingled. This was no ordinary recipe book! She flipped forward to the contents page, and now she understood: All the recipes were for solving problems. Incredible!

One section had recipes for fixing all sorts of bodily problems — everything from baldness (Fuzzbooster Flapjacks) to smelly feet (Un-cheese Cake). Lulu's excitement mounted as she realized that perhaps this book had come to her for a special purpose after all; perhaps it held the solution to her predicament with Varaminta and Torquil! But none of the recipes in this section had the answer.

She flicked through the pages to the next section. This one dealt with "Problems of the Character." Here were recipes such as Cheery Pie, for making miserable people laugh, and Upside-Down Cake, for those who are too serious and sensible. Devil's Food Cake was for people who are extremely righteous, while Cussle Pie and Apstard would make people get their words mixed up and were intended to humiliate the self-satisfied and pompous. Finally, a section titled "Matters of the Heart" had recipes for falling in and out of love.

Lulu had to struggle not to laugh out loud. Her

mind was abuzz with ideas. Just imagine, she thought, what I'll be able to do if these really work! For a moment she paused at the Matters of the Heart recipes. What if she made something to give Dad, to make him fall out of love with Varaminta? But that seemed scary. She didn't know what she was getting into and found she couldn't stomach the idea of experimenting on Dad in such a way. Besides, what about Torquil and all the nasty little schemes he kept getting away with? He'd just keep on getting away with them, wouldn't he? No, it was the Problems of the Character recipes she should concentrate on, to be administered to the Le Bones themselves. Eagerly she searched the pages to see if there was anything for making cruel people kind. Humble Pie was supposed to make brash, boastful people become meek and lowly. An amusing idea . . . but somehow it didn't seem to go far enough. If the effect wore off, they'd soon be back to their old wicked ways. And what if it didn't, and she was stuck living with two humble people saying sorry all the time? She barely knew which was worse. But then Lulu turned the page.

Truth Cookies

For those who tell lies,
who trick others by withholding the truth

a few strands of saffron   *1 cup ground dried sun beans*

1 tablespoon sunflower petals *1 cup ground Asha Vahishta nuts*

1 cup of Reasons   *2 tablespoons Idzumo honey*

6 crow's eggs   *1 tablespoon sunflower seeds*

¾ cup camel's butter

This was irresistible. Perfect for both of them! Torquil the trickster and Varaminta the two-faced gold digger. Yes, the Truth Cookies might just expose them for who they really were, and once that happened, there was no way Dad would tolerate them a moment longer. The Le Bones would be out. Perhaps Lulu would even get Mum-in-Muddy-Wellies back. . . .

But then Lulu read through the ingredients again properly. Asha Vahishta nuts? Dried sun beans? What on earth were they? Where did you get crow's eggs and camel's butter? And one cup of reasons; not raisins, but reasons? Her heart sank. Desperately

she turned back to the introduction and read on —
hoping it might tell her where to get these things:

If you've ever eaten salad and wondered why you
were sleepy afterward, then here is your answer:
Lettuce is governed by the tranquil Moon. Carrots
have their eyesight-enhancing reputation for
good reason; they are governed by Mercury, a
planet with the power to strengthen the brain
(and the eyes). It may not surprise you, therefore, that fiery Nettles, Onions, and Mustard
are all governed by red-hot Mars. Sun plants
strengthen the heart, the seat of one's con-
science. Jupiter plants make you jovial, while
gloomy Saturnine ones can have the opposite
effect. Roses are red, violets are blue, but both
lovely flowers are governed by the love planet,
Venus. She can put a lump in the throat (the
Adam's apple!) and butterflies in your stomach.

A further passage described how the various parts
of the body are governed by different signs of the
zodiac, and therefore their ruling planets. And

the introduction finished by explaining that many other ingredients, like those of dairy, fowl, or insect origin, derive their powers from alternative sources, ones that ancient myths and legends often reveal.

Fascinated though she was, Lulu grew increasingly frustrated. She hadn't found anything to tell her where she was supposed to get the ingredients. She sighed and closed the book; it had to be a joke. No big surprise, she thought. It explained why this wasn't the most famous cookbook in the world. As if in response to this thought, the book fell open in her lap at a new page.

WARNING

These recipes work. In the wrong hands, they may be harmful. This book has come to you because it was meant for you, and no one else. Keep it where no one will ever find it. You have inherited a gift; use it wisely.

Lulu's hopes soared once again. If the book really was meant for her, as Mister O had suggested, if it had always been destined to fall magically into her hands, then maybe something similar would happen with the ingredients.

As Lulu closed the book again, a slip of paper, yellowed and frayed at the edges, fell from inside it and floated to the floor at her feet. She picked it up. Drawn on it was a series of symbols:

It had to be a coded message! And in what looked like . . . Egyptian hieroglyphs? As she tucked the slip back inside *The Apple Star*, Lulu felt a little thrill. Time to raid the library, she decided.

A Carob Bar

"Hey, Noodle," said Dad, on the phone. "How'd it go yesterday?"

Lulu knew that Varaminta was listening on the phone upstairs, as she always did; she could tell from the white noise on the line. Varaminta was still furious at Lulu for ruining her plans to Barbie-fy her. But she had also made it very clear that she did not want Lulu's dad to know what had happened; it would not reflect well on Varaminta at all, especially as he had warned her that beauty salons were not Lulu's idea of fun. Though Lulu had no intention of telling him — Dad would be angry at her behavior too — she thought it would be fun to make Varaminta a little nervous.

"Oh, great, Dad," she gushed. "Unbelievable, in fact!"

Dad sounded surprised. "That good, huh? Oh, you don't know how happy I am to hear you say that! To be honest, I wasn't too sure it would be your kind of thing. . . ."

Lulu stifled a giggle. "Oh, it's my kind of thing, all right. Couldn't be more gorgeously so!"

Dad laughed. "Well! So, what did you have done, then?"

"Many Cures," said Lulu.

"A manicure, lovely," said Dad. "What else?"

"Well, it's amazing what can be done with wax. . . ."

"Ooh, sounds painful!"

"Not at all," said Lulu. "I did something a bit different with it. I —"

Click-click! went the line, as Varaminta pretended she was only now picking up the other phone. "Mikey darling, is that you?"

★ ★ ★

"She took you where?" gasped Frenchy on Monday morning.

"A beauty salon," repeated Lulu.

Frenchy burst out laughing. "Oh, Lu, that's like taking a vegetarian to a steak house!"

"At least Aileen's taking me to the movies this Friday," said Lulu. "She felt sorry for me. You're invited too. But, French, there's something else. . . .

I can't talk about it here, it's secret. I have to *show* you at home. Can you come over on Saturday too?"

Usually, Lulu was picked up from school by Aileen on Mondays, but Frenchy's mum picked her up that afternoon, at Aileen's request. When Lulu arrived home, Aileen wasn't in the kitchen. Lulu went to the bottom of the stairs and called. "Aileen?"

"She's not here," called Torquil, appearing at the top of the stairs.

"Oh, why?" said Lulu. "Is she sick?"

"Nah," grinned Torquil. "She's gone. Said to say 'g'day' to ya!"

Lulu felt the blood drain from her face. "What do you mean, *gone*? Is she taking a vacation?"

Torquil cackled. "No, doofus, she took a hike. Vroom! Finito."

"There's no way," said Lulu. "She wouldn't just —" She broke off, her throat catching, and went through the open door to the sitting room. This had to be some kind of joke.

Varaminta was lounging amid a cloud of pillows, a copy of *Chow!* magazine on her lap. She looked up and coolly announced, "Torquil's right, Louisa. I'm afraid Aileen left."

Lulu stared at her, a lump forming in her throat. "You got rid of her, didn't you?" she said quietly.

Varaminta shut her eyes for a moment, the way teachers do when they want to show extreme patience with a complete idiot. "No, Louisa, she went of her own accord."

Lulu stepped forward. "You're punishing me — and her!" she said, her voice getting louder. "It's because of what happened on Saturday, isn't it?"

Varaminta stood up. "Don't be ridiculous, child," she snapped. "She wanted to go. It might seem sudden to you, but ah! these girls, that's how they are. Such silly, flighty little things." She flapped her hands, making her jewelry and nail polish shimmer.

By now Lulu's face was wet with tears. "You're lying, you're lying!" she sobbed. "Aileen wouldn't just leave like that, I know she wouldn't! She's taking me to the movies, she wouldn't just —"

"Ha!" interrupted Varaminta. "What makes you think you're so important to her? She's a grown adult; she doesn't have to ask your permission to do anything."

Lulu ran to the kitchen phone, and dialed Aileen's cell number; it was switched off. She tried the home number and got the answering machine. "Aileen, are you there? Pick up, Aileen, it's me, Lulu. . . . Aileen, will you please call me back? It's really important!"

As she hung up, she turned to see Varaminta smirking in the doorway, hands on hips. "I found a replacement," said Varaminta. "Her name's Grodmila, and she's from Moldenia. Excellent references; she starts tomorrow. Your father thinks she sounds perfect too. I do hope you'll try to control your rebellious nature, be civil toward her, and not drive her away like you did Aileen."

As Lulu curled up in bed that night, she felt the familiar knot twist and tighten inside her. Was there no part of her life Varaminta and Torquil weren't determined to ruin? "At least I've got *The Apple Star*," she whispered to Grainy-Christmas-Mum. "No Aileen and no Mum-in-Muddy-Wellies, but I do have that book. And I'm going to find those ingredients and use it, whatever it takes!"

★ ★ ★

Grodmila from Moldenia had a shiny red face and a large, hairy mole on her chin. She spoke almost no English, except things like "I vont to clean here now," as soon as anything was slightly out of place. She vacuumed constantly, wielding the machine like a weapon of mass destruction. Everything she cooked was boiled to death and very watery. Torquil usually managed to get takeout, no doubt thanks to his cat-finding reward money and bogus Mutant Droid Limited Edition funds. And Varaminta ate out, if she ate at all. It was only Lulu who had to face the gristly meatballs and soapy soup. Worst of all, Grodmila never, ever smiled. Lulu struggled to think of a candy joyless enough to compare her to, but eventually decided she was a carob bar. A carob bar is a chocolate bar that's not made of chocolate — a poor substitute. The first — and only — time Lulu tried a carob bar, its pointlessness had puzzled and depressed her for the rest of the day.

Aileen didn't call back that evening. Or the day after, or the day after that. Lulu tried calling again and again, but Aileen never picked up or answered the messages.

★ ★ ★

"Hey, Noodle," said Dad into the phone. "I heard about Aileen. I'm so sorry."

"She didn't go, Dad, she was pushed," said Lulu.

"Oh no, love, that's not what —"

"It's true, it has to be," Lulu interrupted. "You know Aileen, she wouldn't just go like that!"

Dad sighed. "I know, it's very disappointing —"

"*Disappointing?!*" gasped Lulu.

"Love, just listen to me for a minute . . . apparently Aileen confided in Varaminta once that her new boyfriend didn't think she should be doing housework."

What boyfriend? And try as she might, Lulu couldn't imagine Aileen "confiding" in Varaminta. "She never said anything to me," she told Dad.

"Noodle, she wouldn't necessarily . . . anyway, you know Aileen's been planning to do this psychology course . . ."

"Part-time! She'd still have time to work for us!"

"The point is, it does all sort of fit. Minty says her

heart just hasn't been in her work these past couple of weeks. She singed some ironing the other day, apparently, a very expensive blouse . . ."

"She wouldn't just go, Dad," insisted Lulu. "Not without saying good-bye!"

"I admit it is sudden, but I'm sure we'll hear from her. She probably just wanted to spare your feelings."

"Look, Varaminta's lying, Dad! She —"

Click! "Mikey?"

"Hello, Minty."

"Dahling," drawled Varaminta. "I simply have to discuss the wedding guest list with you; it absolutely can't wait."

"Yes, love. Look, I tell you what, Noodle; I'll try calling Aileen myself. Okay?"

"Promise?"

"Promise."

"Mikey, I've only got a minute," said Varaminta. "Lulu darling? I'm so sorry you're upset; we'll have another little chat in a moment, all right, sweetie?"

Lulu hung up in disgust. "Another little chat" indeed!

Bubble Gum Pop!

"Just wait till you see this!" whispered Lulu, pulling Frenchy by her arm into her bedroom. She closed the door firmly. Since the beauty salon disaster, Lulu had not been allowed to have any visitors, but she had managed to smuggle Frenchy in through the side door. Fortunately Torquil was at his weekend karate lesson, and Lulu was relying on Waxia to keep Varaminta occupied downstairs with floral arrangements and seating plans.

Frenchy sat on the bed and took out a piece of bubble gum. Lulu turned on the radio to drown out any sounds and went to take the book from its hiding place. It was the perfect spot. Torquil couldn't possibly know that there had once been a fireplace in her room that had been removed to make space for her dresser. Near the floor, there was now an air vent, and it was behind this that Lulu was hiding *The Apple Star*.

Clutching it to her chest, she turned solemnly to her friend.

"I'm not supposed to show this to anyone, you know, but I can't do it alone. You have to swear to keep this secret."

"I swear," said Frenchy, eyeing the book eagerly. "Come on, lemme see! I've been dying of curiosity all week."

"Cross your heart and hope to die?"

"Stick a needle in my eye, *c'mon*, Lu! It's gotta be the mother of all secrets for you to hold out on me like this all week!"

"Interesting choice of words," said Lulu, a smile playing on her lips. She presented the book with a flourish, then bounced onto the bed next to Frenchy, barely able to contain herself. "You won't believe how I got this, French. First I ran away from the beauty salon on my birthday . . ."

Frenchy blew a bubble and popped it. "You didn't!"

"Yeah, I know it was crazy, but . . . then there was this really weird book shop, and I just felt sort of drawn to it."

Frenchy chewed furiously on her bubble gum as she studied the book, and Lulu explained everything that had happened in the shop where books found people, not the other way around. She guided Frenchy through the different sections in *The Apple Star* and their strange recipes for dealing with problems of the body, of the character, and of the heart.

"And, French, check out the inscription on the title page," said Lulu. "You won't believe it."

Frenchy read it. "Oh boy!" she breathed. "Do you think it's really from *your* mum?"

Lulu sat back on her heels and gazed at the Grainy-Christmas-Mum photo. "I'm still not sure what to think," she said slowly. "But here's the thing," she added, turning to Frenchy. "There's a recipe in that book for something called Truth Cookies. Just think, French. They make the eater *tell the truth*!"

Frenchy's eyebrows rose above her glasses. "You mean —"

"Torquil and Varaminta, exactly. If Dad hears the truth from them, well, there's no way he'll want to marry Varaminta." Lulu's excitement grew. "I might even be able to get Aileen back. I just *know* she only left because of Varaminta. . . ."

"Lu —"

". . . Then there's all my mum things that Torquil's got. You see how brilliant it is? This one recipe could change everything!"

Frenchy rested the book in her lap and raised her hands. "Lu, wait a minute. How do you know this is all for real?"

Lulu beamed at her. "Just look at the introduction."

Frenchy turned the page and read. "*Whoa.* This is wild! All this stuff about the evening star, the apples, nymphs, plants, and everything?"

"I know," said Lulu. "But here's where it gets even more mysterious. Take a look at those ingredients. You can't buy that stuff — not in any normal store! But I've found a clue that I think might help." She pulled another book, this one about ancient Egypt, from under her bed. "I got it from the library." She opened the book to reveal the frayed, yellow piece of paper with the hieroglyphs. Lulu had written letters alongside the symbols:

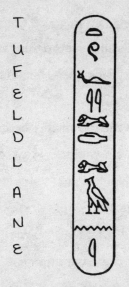

T
U
F
E
L
D
L
A
N
E

Frenchy took the sheet and knitted her brow.

"It wasn't all that easy," said Lulu. "It's not like they had an alphabet the way we do. . . ."

Frenchy went on frowning.

". . . That was the best I could come up with. . . ."

Frenchy looked up slowly. "Tufeldlane?"

Lulu sighed. "I know. Doesn't mean anything, does it? At least, it's not in the dictionary. It's gobbledygook! Or a foreign language . . . I don't know."

Frenchy adjusted her glasses and studied the hieroglyphs, chewing vigorously. She checked the letters to see if Lulu had made a mistake; she hadn't. A pale balloon emerged from her face and then collapsed on her nose. "Okay," she announced, stringing bits of gum back into her mouth. "I've got an idea. What if it's not all one word? I mean, look, that last part could be 'lane.'"

"Oh yeah!" gasped Lulu. "Hey, maybe it's an address! Hopefully an English one, hopefully a London one . . ."

"Exactly what I was thinking," said Frenchy. "Tufeld Lane. Can you look it up on a map?"

Lulu disappeared to her father's study and soon returned, happily waving a battered old street map of London. Most of North West London fell on the floor as they opened the book. Ignoring it, they turned hurriedly to the index at the back. "Tufnell Park Road, Tufton Road . . . ," read Lulu. She sighed heavily. "No Tufeld Lane."

"Hang on!" Frenchy grabbed Lulu's arm. "Look, if it is an address . . . well, it should have a street number, shouldn't it? The 'T-U' at the beginning. Perhaps that's really two. That would make it Number Two Feld Lane."

Lulu blinked. "But . . . you changed the letters. That's cheating."

"Not if they're using the hieroglyph that makes the closest sound, it isn't."

Lulu brightened. "Well, that would make sense." She grabbed the street map and flipped through to the Fs in the index. "Huh. No Feld Lane."

"Hmm," said Frenchy.

Lulu ran her finger down the hieroglyph reference again. "That 'E.' Those two little flags, or whatever they are, can also mean a 'y' sound, or a double 'e' sound. Filed . . . feeld . . ."

Pop! went Frenchy. "Field! You've got it. Two Field Lane, there's your address!"

"Of course! Oh, French, you're a genius!" Lulu consulted the index again. And there, right at the bottom of the page, was Field Lane. Even better, it was only about half a mile away.

"Well, let's go find it right now!" said Frenchy.

Boiled Cabbage

The two girls paused under a large oak tree to catch their breath. "So far, so good!" Lulu managed to whisper. They had left the radio still playing and snuck out the side door, making sure the kitchen window was open for their return.

Lulu checked the map again. Field Lane was just two blocks away on the other side of a cricket field. A game was in progress, so the girls kept near the shadows under the trees around the edge. They didn't want to attract the attention of the extra players; some of Lulu's dad's friends might be among them. They took a shortcut onto Field Lane. What sort of place would it be? Lulu wondered, as they quickened their pace toward Number Two. Fantastic images filled her mind. She pictured a crumbling mansion alongside the canal, where modern-day pirates with Day-Glo hair and lots of tattoos smuggled mysterious cargo in through a large, gothic gate — like Traitor's Gate at the Tower of London. Then there'd be a courtyard where exotic livestock like llamas and camels were milked. And extraordinary plants would be everywhere, bearing bizarrely shaped fruit and flowers with intoxicating scents and iridescent colors. She could barely contain her excitement as they passed the diminishing numbers: eight, six, four . . . two!

"Oh." It was the windows she noticed first: boarded up with panels of plywood. Nettles as high as her nose. A broken path, a rotten gate. Apparently, no one had lived in this house for a very long time. It was more than Lulu could bear. That magical somebody — the one person who might be able to solve all her problems — was gone. Moved away . . . perhaps even dead.

The book would remain a mystery forever.

They both stood in silence for a moment. Then Frenchy gently took Lulu's arm. "Come on, Lu. We'd better get back before they send out a search party."

"NO!" snapped Lulu, standing her ground. She lunged at the wooden panel that covered the front door and banged on it, her face wet with tears. "HELLO! ANYBODY HOME?"

"Lu! Sshh!" hissed Frenchy. "Are you crazy? It's barred. No one can get in or out!"

"Maybe there's a secret entrance. Around the back!"

But there was no access to the back of the house, and eventually Lulu allowed herself to be coaxed away. Frenchy picked up speed, and soon Lulu, too, was running as fast as she could, tears streaming into her ears.

★ ★ ★

Back home, they found the window had been closed. Lulu tried the handle of the side door, but it was locked. She went back to the window and tried to push it open, but it was no use. Then she caught sight of Varaminta's glowering face.

Lulu sprang back down to below the level of the sill. "Go!" she hissed to Frenchy. "It's Varaminta, but I don't think she saw you."

Frenchy hesitated. "Are you sure you're okay?"

Lulu wiped her tears away and put on a brave smile. "I'm fine. Honestly. Now go, quickly!" She squeezed Frenchy's arm. "And thanks."

Frenchy nodded, wide-eyed behind her glasses.

Lulu had to think fast to invent an explanation, but Varaminta wasn't impressed. She just stood tapping her foot, arms folded, while Lulu stammered and faltered. Torquil was back and leaned against the door frame behind his mother, smirking.

"It was an emergency," Lulu insisted. "I called out, I thought you heard me."

"And your friend's mother just happened to be parked on our street when she discovered her car wouldn't start," said Varaminta sarcastically.

"Liar, liar, pants on fire!" taunted Torquil.

"She was . . . visiting a friend down the street," added Lulu. "All she needed was a little push. . . ."

"Flame-grilled whopper," said Torquil.

This sent Lulu over the edge. "Well, you'd know all about lies and whoppers, wouldn't you, Torquil. And *fishy* tales!"

"Watch it!" hissed Torquil, his eyes narrowed. Poochie looked up from his dish of chicken livers and growled.

"I'm not listening to any more of this," snarled Varaminta. "You're grounded for another week.

And . . . let me see . . . this diet of yours; how's it going?"

"I'm not on a diet," said Lulu.

"No, I thought not. Well, since being grounded seems to have little impact on your behavior, perhaps a change of diet is needed too. I'm sure Grodmila will rise to the occasion. Torquil, any suggestions?"

"Hmm . . . ," said Torquil, rubbing his chin, clearly examining in his mind the worst of Grodmila's cooking.

Don't say boiled cabbage, don't say boiled cabbage, willed Lulu.

"I've got it!" said Torquil. "Boiled cabbage!"

Varaminta smirked. "Excellent. Seven days' worth of boiled cabbage, then. That'll knock her into shape!"

Lulu's heart sank.

★ ★ ★

The noise vibrated all the way down the sludge-green walls of the school hallway.

"*UUUURRRP!*"

"Lu!"

"Oops, sorry," said Lulu. "I can't help it. It's all the boiled cabbage."

"What?"

"Every night for a week. Boiled cabbage. It's my punishment for going out with you on Saturday. And I'm still grounded."

"Oh, Lu, you poor thing," said Frenchy. "Listen, I'll smuggle in extra sandwiches for you, how's that?"

"That — *uurrp* — would be fantastic!" said Lulu.

"But, listen, big news," added Frenchy excitedly, grabbing Lulu's arm and lowering her voice. "I've been dying to tell you! I looked at the street map at home last night, and guess what? You know how Field Lane was at the bottom of a right-hand page in the index?"

"Yes . . ."

"We didn't look over the page, Lu. There are two more!"

"Two more Field Lanes?"

"Yes! We should've looked. Now, listen, one of them is in Hackney, and — guess what — it's right near where my dad lives."

Lulu gasped.

Frenchy paused as some other kids passed by, then whispered, "Listen, I'm staying with him this weekend, so I'm going to investigate."

"Oh no, you're not!" cried Lulu, indignantly.

"What do you mean?"

"Not by yourself, you're not. I'm coming with you! Invite me for a sleepover."

"But you're grounded!"

Lulu scowled at her. Frenchy raised her hands and laughed. "Okay, okay."

With a high five, Lulu sealed the agreement. "*UUUURRRP!*" she said.

Samosa Sleepover

Varaminta was out at a wedding-dress fitting that evening, so Lulu didn't have a chance to raise the issue of the sleepover. She spent much of the evening gazing at the Grainy-Christmas-Mum photo, trying to dream up a way she might wangle permission.

Coming home on the bus on Tuesday, she had to admit she still hadn't come up with a decent plan. She wondered if she shouldn't wait until Thursday to ask, and be a complete angel until then. She racked her brains for ways to earn extra brownie points, but by the time she was heading up the garden path, her prospects still seemed pretty hopeless. Whatever she dreamed up — being super-nice to Torquil by letting him con her; making a show of fondness toward Poochie; pretending to be really interested in Varaminta's book — she realized would only make her hate herself. Besides, Varaminta would probably become suspicious. But there *had* to be a way. The more Lulu thought about those Truth Cookies, the more she felt they were the only solution to her problems.

Then she walked into her room. Or what was left of it — it had shrunk to almost half its original size. A brand-new wall gleamed mockingly at her. Her bed practically filled the room, and she had to squeeze between it and the desk to get to the other side, which was entirely taken up by the dresser. This, at least, was still in the same place. Lulu dashed over to check that *The Apple Star* was still safely tucked behind the air vent; it was. What she had left of the Wodge of Stuff, too, was mercifully untouched. But her shelves had been removed, and the contents carelessly dumped in a messy pile on her bed. No sooner had Lulu taken all this in than she heard Varaminta wailing, "Oh, it's all a horrible mistake! I don't know what to do!"

Lulu went out into the hallway where she could hear the voice more clearly; it was coming from the bedroom. "But, Mikey, I told them we weren't going with that plan anymore; I thought they understood! And then I was out for most of the day, and the next thing I knew . . ."

The sneak! thought Lulu, still barely able to believe what had happened. Varaminta had obviously found a way of getting her bathroom extension. Lulu ran to the study and picked up the other phone. "She did it on purpose, Dad, I know she did!"

"Now, Lulu. Varaminta wouldn't —"

"Oh yes, she would, and did, and meant it with bells on!" cried Lulu, to gasps of indignation from Varaminta. "She's doing all this for herself for when she marries you and moves in, not for you — for her and her *Chow!* magazine people! And she won't let me stay at Frenchy's on Friday night."

Dad was quiet for a moment. "Minty?"

"The poor thing's hysterical," said Varaminta.

"I can't say I blame her," said Dad.

Varaminta began whining like an ambulance. "Oh, Mikey, I'm just trying to do the best for your house, for you, darling. It wasn't my fault!"

"All right, all right, I'm not saying it was," said Dad. "Look, I'll be back on Sunday. Lulu? We'll work something out, okay, Noodle? It's probably time we fixed up that attic room, anyway. . . . Now, what's all this about Friday night?"

So Lulu got her sleepover. "It's the least we can do," said Dad. Varaminta didn't care, really; she had her extravagant bathroom extension, after all.

Frenchy's dad wasn't too thrilled, but after Frenchy had called him three times about it, he gave in. The problem was space. "We'll have to share the couch," Frenchy explained to Lulu. "And it's . . . well, you'll see. He paints; there's an awful lot of paint and stuff around. And he doesn't cook, so I hope you like Indian food?"

"I love it!" proclaimed Lulu, hugging her. "It's not cabbage!"

★ ★ ★

The murky cloud of the day was disappearing into the night sky like melting snow. Helped by the bright moonlight, Frenchy and Lulu picked their way across a stretch of vacant land.

"Got the money?" asked Frenchy.

Lulu bit her lip. "Ah. Yes, well . . ."

"You don't?"

"No, I do, it's just . . . it's not very much. Haven't had any allowance for a while."

"Oh, great."

"Well, how do we know what it'll cost, anyway?" hissed Lulu. "Might be a hundred pounds!"

"Okay, okay!" Frenchy reached out and squeezed Lulu's arm.

They fell silent as they continued on their way. Lulu took a deep breath of the cool night air. She couldn't remember the last time she'd seen such a wide expanse of sky, its canopy of stars suspended over her like a magnificent display of Christmas lights. It made everything seem unreal, or more than real, and she found herself imagining that they were two spirits of the night. *The Apple Star*'s words came back to her: "Your star, the one that speaks to you, and only you, across time and space."

She linked arms with Frenchy. "Remember what the book said, French? About letting your star be your guide . . . how do I know which star is mine?"

Frenchy thought for a moment, adjusting her glasses. "Use your intuition, my mum would say. That's how she found our flat. We couldn't afford much at the time, and everything we looked at was terrible. Then Mum saw this house, and she just had a feeling about it. Turned out, the old lady who owned it had been thinking of renting out a flat she owned that her son had just moved out of. She was really kind; she let us rent it really cheaply."

"That was lucky," said Lulu.

"Not luck, Mum doesn't believe in that. You make your own luck, she says. People think too much, she figures; sometimes you just have to go with what you feel. Maybe that's what happened with you and that weird book shop, Lu. Maybe you can do the same with the star."

Lulu gazed skyward again. Along the spilled chalk-dust path of the Milky Way, her eye was drawn to a bright star, with two close companions. It winked at her.

★ ★ ★

Lulu was relieved to find that this Number Two Field Lane wasn't abandoned. But it was disappointingly ordinary; just a typical town house, with a London taxicab parked in the small driveway. She suddenly realized that they didn't know how to tell if they had the right Field Lane; there was, after all, another that they hadn't investigated. What exactly had she expected to find? A big neon sign saying "*The Apple*

Star Supermarket"? She paused for a moment, concentrating her thoughts on the bright star — her star.

"What's up, Lu?" whispered Frenchy.

"Trying to let the star be my guide," she said. "But I think I need a little practice."

"Never mind," hissed Frenchy. "Take a look at that instead." She pulled Lulu closer and pointed to the front door. There, in the middle of the door, was a huge brass knocker with a life-size face on it. The face looked exactly like an Egyptian pharaoh, complete with striped headdress and a funny little beard hanging down like a thick, stubby tail.

"Wow," gasped Lulu. As they moved nearer, Lulu could make out a brass plaque by the doorbell, like the one at the dentist's. She peered closer, then tugged at Frenchy's sleeve. "Check this out!" On the plaque were some hieroglyphs, the same ones that Lulu had found in her book.

The girls exchanged wide-eyed glances. "Oh boy," said Frenchy. "This is the place, all right! Hey, d'you see the name?" Under the hieroglyphs it was engraved MS. C. PATRA.

"C. Patra . . . Cleopatra. Like the Egyptian queen,

get it?" Frenchy nudged Lulu. All the excitement was putting her in a silly mood. "Get it? Huh? Huh?"

"Sshh!" said Lulu. "Stop that! What do we do now?"

"Well, knock, silly."

"Okay, here goes." Lulu lifted the brass beard and let it drop with a dull thud.

Nothing happened. They stared at the knocker. Frenchy peered in the window, trying to see beyond the drawn curtains. "There seems to be a light on in there," she whispered. She sighed and reached for the beard herself, but as she did so, there was a *sloosh*, like a drawer opening, and . . . *the pharaoh opened his eyes.*

The girls squealed with terror; Frenchy grabbed Lulu's hair, Lulu grabbed Frenchy's face, and they stumbled and tumbled backward off the doorstep, crashing into the bushes.

"Password!" demanded the pharaoh.

strange Tea

The girls sat clinging to each other, stunned.

"Password!" said the pharaoh eyes again. Lulu's mind spun. "Uh . . ." What to say: Open sesame? Rumpelstiltskin? Frenchy nudged her and pointed to the book she was clutching, wrapped in a plastic bag.

"Oh yes," said Lulu, standing up and brushing the seat of her jeans. "Ahem. *The Apple Star*," she proclaimed boldly. There was another *sloosh*, and the eyes closed again. A further series of clicks and rumblings, and the door swung open to reveal a large African-looking woman in a billowing purple gown. She had big, dark eyes; the very eyes that had peered through the holes when the pharaoh's eyelids opened, Lulu now realized. She wore dangly earrings in turquoise and amber, and her long black hair was tied back with a flowing red scarf.

"Come in," said the woman in her deep, caramel-coated pharaoh voice.

Lulu hesitated. "Go on!" whispered Frenchy,

nudging her in the small of her back. Lulu stepped forward and Frenchy followed.

"S-sorry to bother you so late . . . ," began Lulu.

The woman smiled. "Oh, we don't worry about that. I'm used to having people come by at the strangest hours." She leaned closer and gave them a knowing wink. "It's always a secret, right?" She held out her hand. "I'm Cassandra. . . ."

"Oh!" said Frenchy, disillusioned.

Cassandra blinked at her. "Is there a problem?"

"No, nothing," said Frenchy hastily. "Um . . . I'm Frenchy. And this is Lulu. Lulu's the one with the . . . thing. Aren't you, Lulu?"

"Uh, yes," said Lulu, waving the book, still shrouded in plastic. She couldn't think of anything else to say. It all seemed so unreal.

"May I see?" said Cassandra. Lulu unwrapped the book and handed it to her. Cassandra put her hand to her mouth. "You really do have it!" she exclaimed. "I've heard of this one, but I've never seen it. Hmm . . ." She held the book close to her face, flicking the pages, absorbing everything eagerly and ushering them into the next room at the same time. "Uh-huh . . . oh! . . . mmm . . ." She looked admiringly at Lulu. "A very special one, this book. Very special indeed."

Suddenly Lulu desperately wanted to ask if Cassandra had known her mother, but it felt silly. What if it was just coincidence that a book, a birthday present from another mum to another Lulu, fell at her feet on her own birthday? But then again, what if it wasn't? Then, before Lulu could get up the courage to say anything, Cassandra said, "Have a seat." She laid *The Apple Star* on a low, round table. "Tea?"

"Oh no, thank you," said Lulu. "I don't like tea."

"You'll like this one," insisted Cassandra, and she swished out of the room.

Lulu and Frenchy sank gratefully into a huge, squishy sofa. Lulu felt a bit like Alice after eating the cake that made her shrink; everything here was so large.

"Do you think she's crazy?" whispered Frenchy.

Lulu giggled nervously. "She'd better not be!" She tried not to think about it, and instead began to take in her surroundings. The room was quite astonishing, not least because of the smell. It smelled like toffee and mud, candles and Christmas, pepper and forests. She could see the candles and guessed the other smells came from the back wall, where rows of big jars stood, like in an old-fashioned candy store. On a table were some brass scales, a large stone bowl, and an enormous open book.

There was a mural on the opposite wall showing a huge palm tree, surrounded by life-size Egyptian figures, humans with animal and bird heads. "See that figure?" Lulu said, pointing out a bird-headed man with a large golden sun disc radiating from the top of his head. "He's in my ancient Egypt book. The sun god, Re."

"Are you sure it's pronounced Ray? I thought it was Ra," said Frenchy. She giggled. "Ray . . . who's that next to him, then? Kevin?"

Lulu chortled. "Yeah, and he's next to Brenda, there!"

They fell silent as Cassandra tinkled toward them with the tea tray. When she had poured the golden liquid into three little glasses, she settled down next to Lulu.

"So! Did you have a particular recipe in mind, Lulu?"

"Yes," said Lulu. She opened the book to the Truth Cookies page and handed it to Cassandra. "This one."

Cassandra clapped a large hand on Lulu's shoulder, making her jump, and proclaimed, "Ah, you have a deceiver in your life!"

"Two, actually," said Frenchy.

Cassandra gently lifted Lulu's chin and gazed at her with her huge, black-rimmed eyes. "Poor child. Tut-tut! Such cruelty you have endured. I can see it in your eyes." She heaved a sigh.

Lulu resisted the urge to giggle. Cassandra was overwhelming; she was so big and lovely in every way, it all added up to rather too much bigness and loveliness for Lulu to know what to do with it.

"So, Truth Cookies . . . a Level Three recipe, it says here," said Cassandra. "As opposed to a simpler Level One recipe, such as the ones dealing with bodily problems. This ranks up with the Matters of the Heart recipes." She turned to Lulu. "You do realize these Level Three recipes are the strongest ones, don't you?"

"Uh, I guess," said Lulu.

"Not to be used for any frivolous purposes," Cassandra warned.

"There's nothing frivolous about this," Frenchy assured her.

"No, I can see that," said Cassandra. "So," she went on, "let's see now . . . camel's butter; very common ingredient, I always carry plenty of that, good stuff, although a bit lumpy. . . . Sun beans and Asha Vahishta nuts; I'll have a look. Do you need the saffron, sunflower seeds, and petals as well?"

"Yes, I do. All these 'sun' things!"

"Absolutely essential!" Cassandra announced passionately, and she stood up and gave a great purple-armed swoop in front of the sun god figure. "All is revealed in the light of the sun," she added dramatically. "Deception lurks only in the shadows!"

"Well, yes, I suppose that's true. . . ." Lulu sipped the sweet, hot tea. It was delicious.

Cassandra swished her way back to the couch. "Of course it's true. Now then, where were we? Crow's eggs, Idzumo honey, both fine, and . . . ah yes, 'reasons.'"

"Is that . . . something I get from you?" asked Lulu. She felt slightly foolish asking the question.

Cassandra smiled, much to Lulu's relief. "No, my dear, those must come from you."

Lulu screwed up her face. "Er — how? I mean, what . . . ?"

Cassandra chuckled. "I will give you some special ink and a pen. With them you must write down your thoughts. As you write, so your reasons will pour onto the page. The reasons why you are unhappy and need the Truth Cookies. Let them dry, then soak them, as with tea. It is this infusion that you add to the recipe."

"Oh," said Lulu, wide-eyed. "Wow."

Cassandra turned to Frenchy. "Now, I'm sorry, Frenchy, but I'll have to ask you to wait in the hall. This part must be conducted in the strictest confidence; it's one of the rules of the book."

Frenchy gulped her tea. "Oh," she said. Awkwardly, she replaced her cup in its saucer and stood up. "Okay," she added hesitantly. "I'll be . . . just out here, then, Lu."

"All right," said Lulu reluctantly. Frenchy was her security blanket, and it felt unnerving to be left alone without her.

"I'm sorry, Lulu," said Cassandra, when Frenchy had left. "But this is absolutely secret. I'm bending the rules as it is, by letting her in at all. So . . . back to business." She stood up and headed toward the back of the room, carrying *The Apple Star* with her.

Lulu stood up too, but suddenly felt light-headed. She didn't know whether it was the lack of sleep, the tea, or all the pungent smells, but as she walked, she had to steady herself by leaning on the furniture. Her vision seemed a little blurry too, but she forced herself onward and followed Cassandra into a smaller room. It was here that she came face-to-face with an Egyptian pharaoh! Lulu rubbed her eyes, looked again, and realized that what she was looking at was not actually a pharaoh but the broad shape of one, complete with golden face and staring eyes, painted all over with birds and suns and lotus flowers. A mummy case! Then Cassandra reached up to grasp a large handle at the side of it, and Lulu felt a lurch in her belly. Was she going to open the coffin?

"NO!" Lulu cried, stepping backward. She felt nauseous. What was going on? Was this some sort of bizarre ritual? Lulu had visions of Cassandra making her dance around a leathery corpse or something horrible. The dizziness got worse, and she found herself wishing she had never come.

"It's all right," Cassandra reassured her. She took Lulu's hand and pulled her closer. Lulu felt the blood drain from her face.

"Come along," said Cassandra.

She's a sorceress! thought Lulu, and now everything fell into place: the strange house, Frenchy banished, the strange tea — drugged, no doubt!

Cassandra drew her closer still. Lulu shut her eyes. *This isn't happening, this isn't happening. . . .* There was a low hum, then a loud sucking noise, and a ghostly chill ran through her. She opened her eyes and was immediately dazzled by a bright light.

"No!" she gasped again, gripped with fear. She wrenched her hand from Cassandra's, turned on her heel, and *whack!* Something hard hit her on the head.

The Sun Egg

"Good heavens, are you all right, dear?" said Cassandra, steadying Lulu gently. Lulu blinked several times and rubbed her head. As her eyes adjusted to the bright light, at last she understood. The "mummy case," she now saw, was just the front of a gigantic walk-in fridge. It was the now-open fridge door that Lulu had banged her head on in her panic to get away.

"Oh! I thought . . ."

Cassandra smiled. "I think your imagination was running away with you. Forgive me, I should have explained. I don't get many customers as young as you!"

Lulu managed a smile. "No, I guess not."

Cassandra put her arm around Lulu's shoulder. "Are you sure you're all right?"

Lulu could feel a small bump forming at the side of her head. She shrugged. "I'll be okay. I feel kind of faint, though. I was a little wobbly on my feet just now."

"Oh, you poor dear! Well, it is awfully late. Are you hungry, perhaps?"

Lulu suddenly realized that she was ravenous. She had been too nervous to eat much of the Indian food at Frenchy's dad's place.

"Yes, I am, actually."

"Do you like eggs?"

"Yes," said Lulu.

Cassandra guided her into the enormous fridge. "Well, take your pick!" There were egg boxes covering an entire wall, from floor to ceiling. They were labeled alphabetically, from ALBATROSS and ALLIGATOR at the top, down to UMBRELLA BIRD and VULTURE at the bottom.

"Wow!" said Lulu. "Are they real?"

"Of course! Extremely rare, though, so I have to be very careful who I bring in here. But perhaps a stork egg isn't quite what you had in mind? How about a piece of antelope cheese? It's very sustaining." She offered Lulu a small wedge from the cheese section.

Lulu wasn't too happy but tried it, anyway. It was tangy and creamy, and definitely made her feel a little stronger. "Oh boy, thanks," she said, licking her fingers. "Makes a nice change from boiled cabbage."

"Boiled cabbage?"

"It's what I've had to eat all week."

Cassandra held her hands up in horror. "No wonder you're feeling faint! Now," she continued, consulting *The Apple Star*, "it's crow's eggs we need, isn't it?"

"Yes." Lulu felt vaguely disappointed that her recipe didn't call for anything quite as exciting as alligator eggs. "Why crow's eggs?" she asked.

Cassandra took down a box, opened it, and picked up one of the small, green, speckled eggs. "You know from your book about the star in the apple. Well, inside here" — she cracked the egg into a small dish, revealing a perfectly round, very yellow yolk — "is a tiny sun. The Inuit people of Canada tell of a time before there was daylight. It was the crow who flew east to find it. He brought them back a ball of sunlight on a length of string. When he let it drop, it shattered into tiny pieces. The fragments of light filled every home, banishing darkness forever more."

Lulu wrinkled her nose. "But isn't that just a myth?"

Cassandra looked her squarely in the eye. "Never dismiss the symbolic; it is there for a reason. It has meaning and truth . . . of a kind. Have faith, my dear! Now . . ." She turned to browse along the opposite wall of the fridge. This was full of butter, cream, and milk, and this time the labels said things like ELEPHANT, HIPPOPOTAMUS, and ZEBRA. Just about everything, in fact, except "cow." Cassandra picked out some camel's butter, and they returned to the sweet, spicy warmth of the room. Cassandra consulted the recipe again, climbed a ladder up to the "A" section of the shelves, and took down a big jar of creamy white granules and tipped some into her brass scales.

"Asha Vahishta nuts. Only found in India. There is an ancient saying that only true words are spoken after eating this nut." She finished measuring and replaced the jar. "But its effect does not last long enough by itself. For that, we need the next ingredient . . . honey. I have quite a collection." She led Lulu to the honey cabinet. The honeys were every shade of gold and red, and some were even green and purple.

Lulu gave a low whistle. "Purple honey? Wow!"

Cassandra removed a deep-red jar marked IDZUMO and brought it to the table. "This one is made from the flowers of the legendary Japanese Talking Tree." She opened it and dipped in a spoon. "Here, have a taste!"

"A talking tree?" said Lulu, taking the spoon.

"Of course," said Cassandra matter-of-factly. "All plants talk, didn't you know that?" She heaved a sigh. "Alas! People never hear them anymore!" For a moment she seemed lost in thought.

Lulu swallowed the fragrant honey. "That's . . . mmm, lovely! Uh, so if all plants talk, what's so special about this Japanese Talking Tree, then?"

Cassandra blinked. "Hmmm? Oh, because it's so much noisier than the others, of course! It's gorgeous-looking — beautiful blossom — but it babbles all day long; really most irritating." She went on to make up little packages of the ground yellow sun beans, saffron, sunflower seeds, and dried sunflower petals, and put everything, together with a long, old-fashioned dip pen and a pot of iridescent red ink, into a burlap bag. "Now try to keep these things cool, and use them as soon as possible; the fresher they are, the more potent they'll be. And be very careful where you store them; don't put them in the fridge! You don't want anyone else finding them, do you?"

Lulu put her hand to her mouth. "Oh no, of course!"

"Now, there was one more thing. What was it?" Cassandra flicked her fingers the way adults do to switch on their brains.

"I think that's everything," said Lulu, doubtfully.

Cassandra peered again at the recipe. "Ah yes, that's it!" She delved into a drawer and pulled out a huge, wispy feather. "You'll need this, an ostrich feather."

Lulu was sure she'd seen no mention of ostrich feathers in the ingredients list, and try as she might, she couldn't imagine feathers enhancing the flavor. But Cassandra pressed the feather into her hand, adding in a conspiratorial tone, "It's the symbol of Maat, the Egyptian goddess of truth. Wave it over the mixture before you bake; you must use the words too. It's in the footnotes; it'll make all the difference." She shook Lulu's hand three times as she said, "Don't forget!"

"Oh, I won't!" said Lulu. She couldn't help doing the three-shakes thing as well. She put the feather in the burlap bag and fumbled around in her purse for some change.

Cassandra smiled and patted her on the shoulder. "Never mind about that," she said. "Another time. You may need me again. Here's my card; I can deliver, you know." She let Frenchy back in and began blowing out candles. "Wait a minute, it's late — I'll give you a ride home." She handed *The Apple Star* back to Lulu. "Fascinating, thank you for bringing it."

"We found the introduction a bit mysterious, really," said Lulu. "All that stuff about gardens and nymphs."

"Ah, the Garden of the Hesperides," said Cassandra, blowing out some more candles. "Do you know the story from Greek mythology? Heracles — you probably know him better as Hercules — had to get the golden apples from the garden and bring them to Eurystheus. He was warned not to pick the apples himself but to get Atlas to do it for him. Then there was the small matter of slaying the hundred-headed dragon that guarded the tree! A test of physical courage . . . but without his cunning, Heracles would have been nothing."

"This sounds familiar," said Frenchy. "He out-smarted Atlas, didn't he?"

"That's right," said Cassandra, leading them into the hallway. "Atlas, whose job it was to hold up the sky, passed his burden on to Heracles and picked the apples. But then Atlas tried to trick Heracles into continuing to hold up the sky while he took the apples to Eurystheus — secretly, Atlas didn't plan on coming back."

"What did Heracles do?" asked Lulu.

"He pretended to agree but asked Atlas to hold the sky for a moment so he could put a pad on his head." Cassandra clapped loudly. "Ha! Atlas fell for it, and Heracles made off with the apples. So you see, Lulu, you must take great care," she added, drawing closer. "You have all the ingredients for solving your problem. But you must match your enemy in cunning; that is something no one else can do for you. Come, let's go."

One Cup of Reasons

Cassandra's London taxi turned out to be anything but ordinary. It had luxurious blue velvet seats, and provisions for a midnight feast!

"Open the cabinet in front of you," called Cassandra from the driver's seat. Lulu reached over and pulled a knob where there would once have been a flip-down seat. A little light came on, and a shelf extended forward. On it was an assortment of lacquered boxes.

"Open the one marked 'Shut-Up Shortbread,'" said Cassandra. "You can help yourselves; it temporarily silences both voice and footsteps. Very useful for sneaking silently back into bed."

"Oh, cool, thanks!" said Frenchy.

"Is it your recipe?" asked Lulu, opening the box.

"Yes," said Cassandra. "I dabble; I'm not in the same league as your book's author, Ambrosia May, though! Can't do anything that affects people's behavior, or emotions, try as I might. That is what's so special about *The Apple Star*."

The two girls took a piece each. It was the lightest shortbread Lulu had ever tasted.

"So, Lu," said Frenchy. "How does it feel to be a modern-day Heracles?"

Lulu laughed. "Great, as long as I can really get rid of that hundred-headed dragon I live with. It *feels* like a hundred of her, anyway, with all those pictures everywhere."

"Right," agreed Frenchy. "And Torquil's your Atlas, the trickster."

"You're right there," said Lulu, her voice disappearing.

"Oh! That was quick!" said Frenchy.

They looked at each other and laughed. Or rather, their shoulders went up and down, and their mouths widened, but they made not a sound.

Cassandra pulled over. "Here we are; better let you walk this last stretch. But be quick; it doesn't last very long!"

The girls stepped out of the cab and waved. Lulu felt as if she were literally walking on air.

"Good-bye, Frenchy," said Cassandra. "And good

luck with the dreaded Le Bones, Lulu. Take care you don't break those eggs!"

Silently, the girls entered the house with the key Frenchy had smuggled out. Silently, they climbed the stairs and let themselves into the flat. Silently, Lulu walked into the coat tree — and silently *almost* broke the crow's eggs. "Aarrgh!" she screamed silently. Finally the two of them silently undressed and slid under the covers.

There was something odd about Cassandra's last words. . . . What was it? Lulu wondered as she drifted off to sleep.

". . . Good-bye . . . good luck . . ."

Then Lulu realized she had never mentioned the "dreaded Le Bones" by name to Cassandra.

★ ★ ★

The telephone rang. And rang and rang. Lulu grunted and pulled the blankets over her head.

"Uuurggh!" moaned Frenchy, instantly yanking them back to her end of the couch. Frenchy's dad burst through in pajamas, crunching on takeout containers as he crossed the room.

"Hello?" he croaked.

"Oh-o-o-oh!" groaned Frenchy, turning over crossly.

"Uh, who? . . . Oh, hello . . . yeah, she's here. Oh, I'm sorry, I didn't know. Yeah, of course . . . we'll be over right away . . . sorry. Good-bye." He turned to Lulu. "That was your stepmum. Says you were supposed to be home an hour ago?"

Lulu squinted at him. "What time is it?"

"Ten o'clock."

"Oh, shoot, sorry, I forgot!"

★ ★ ★

Varaminta gave her a long, hard look. "You're a scheming little minx, aren't you? Don't think I don't know what you're up to!" she snarled.

Lulu flushed bright red, in spite of herself. She can tell . . . ?

"You thought you'd sneak in another day away with your friend, I suppose?" Varaminta went on. "Well, I'm not that easily fooled. As far as I'm concerned, you're still grounded."

Oh, is that all? thought Lulu, with immense relief.

"No, honest, it's just that I . . . ," she began. She slipped out of the shoulder straps of her backpack, which carried all the things from Cassandra.

Varaminta seized it — "Now get out of my sight!" — and she flung it across the hall. Lulu's eyes turned to saucers and she skidded across the shiny floor and caught the backpack just in time. She began to climb the stairs.

Torquil leaned on the banisters. "*She did it on purpose, Dad, I know she did!*" he mimicked, in a high-pitched voice. Lulu glared at him.

"Oh yes," Varaminta went on. "And to make up for that little piece of meddling, you are to do some polishing. I've acquired some items for improving the look of the kitchen, but they are very tarnished. It's all on the kitchen table, and Grodmila is under strict instructions not to help. Torquil, Poochie, and I are going out. When we return at five o'clock, I want to see my face in every single item."

Can't imagine why, thought Lulu, but she ran upstairs, elated. A little polishing wouldn't take too long. Then, with Varaminta and Torquil out of the house, she would have the perfect opportunity to make the cookies. At last everything was falling beautifully into place. This time next week, she thought, my nightmare will be over. Lulu put her backpack on the bed and began pulling out its contents until she found the pen and the bottle of red ink.

"Reasons, reasons, oh boy, have I got reasons!" she muttered to the Grainy-Christmas-Mum photo as she heard the front door slam. She swept her desk clean, sending a cascade of pencil shavings and candy wrappers to the floor. Then she found a scrap of paper and wrote:

1. Torquil is the meanest, most horrid, twisted liar. And he's tricky, greedy, and wicked.
2. Varaminta. Same thing. And she's a gold digger.
3. Plus, she got rid of Aileen.
4. If Dad knew what they were really like, he wouldn't like them anymore, and he wouldn't marry Varaminta, and they'd leave us forever.
5. Or he wouldn't like Varaminta anymore, and Torquil will have to go if she goes.
P.S. AND THE DOGLET TOO.

Bread and Stuff

When Lulu walked into the kitchen a few minutes later, her jaw dropped. There were about thirty picture frames and a jewelry box containing heaven only knew how many things. Silver trays, silver cutlery, and silver candlesticks, and a pile of copper cooking pots, all stacked on the table. All black with tarnish. Varaminta must have bought them cheaply, thought Lulu; she knew Dad hadn't want to spend any money on the kitchen. Lulu calculated that she would need at least an hour to make the cookies, and another half hour for them to cool so she could pack them away and hide them. That meant that she would have to start on them by three o'clock, and it was already past twelve.

"You in trabble," said Grodmila, shaking her head.

Lulu sighed heavily and plopped herself down in front of the pile of tarnished metal. She picked up the bottle of silver polish and went to work. After half an hour she was hot, her arms ached, and she had only finished six picture frames. She wiped her brow, leaving a grimy stain. This was hopeless! Her mind ticked over as she gazed numbly out the window. A light breeze tinkled through the wind chimes, and Lulu found herself imagining it was the voices of the trees. Cassandra! Of course. Cassandra would come to her rescue.

★ ★ ★

"If you're asking me to make the cookies for you, the answer is no," said Cassandra firmly.

"But —"

"I'm very sorry, but it's one of the rules. It wouldn't work, anyway. Everything could backfire if anyone but you made those cookies. That's why there's a warning in the book."

Lulu, sitting on the toilet lid with the cordless phone, let out a heavy groan which echoed all around the bathroom.

"You okay?" called Grodmila.

"Uh, yes . . . be down in a minute," Lulu yelled.

"Look, maybe I can help in some other way," said Cassandra. "Why can't you make them?"

Lulu explained about the polishing, and Cassandra

151

said, "Oh, is that all? I've got just the stuff. I'll be with you in half an hour. Look out for me."

"Hang on, I need to give you —" said Lulu, but Cassandra had already hung up.

". . . the address."

Lulu stared at the phone. Cassandra, she decided, was like that box of locoum Dad once brought back from a trip to Istanbul. It was Turkish delight, he'd said, but Lulu found it unlike any other Turkish delight she had ever tasted. It was exotic and mysterious and wonderful.

Half an hour later, Lulu left the kitchen and knelt on the window seat in the front room.

"You hev to clean," ordered Grodmila. "Varaminta very enkry."

"I'm just taking a break, Grodmila," said Lulu.

The Moldenian shook her head as she walked away. "You in trabble!"

Lulu stuck her tongue out at Grodmila behind her back, then turned around just in time to see a black taxi drawing to a halt outside. Cassandra emerged, dressed in a flowing red robe, much like the purple one she'd worn the evening before. She wafted over to the open window and handed Lulu a small package.

"Use this," she whispered. "You'll be amazed!"

Lulu clutched the package. "Thank you!"

"I'm sorry I can't do more," said Cassandra. "Oh, but here . . ." — she fished around in her sacklike shoulder bag and took out another, larger package — "I thought you might be hungry."

Lulu peeked inside; it was some sort of fresh, cheesy bread. "Ooh, thanks! It smells lovely."

Cassandra gave her hand a squeeze. "And remember, *you* are not to blame for all this. You're not the guilty one. Keep telling yourself that."

"How did you know that's how Varaminta makes me feel?"

Cassandra raised her hands. "I know the type. The world's full of them. They'll make you believe everything's your fault!" Her big black-rimmed eyes widened as she whispered, "It's what gives them power. Don't let her have it over you, or it will rot you from the inside out." She turned to leave.

Lulu felt goose bumps spread up her arms. "Cassandra?" she gasped quickly.

Cassandra stopped and turned. "Yes?"

"Did you know my mum?" blurted Lulu. "Her . . . her name was Heather Baker. The inscription in *The Apple Star* said, well . . . oh, never mind, I'm being silly. . . ."

Cassandra stepped back toward her. "Of course you're not being silly!" She paused, then reached over and took Lulu's hand. "Your mother was a very special person." Then she put a finger to her lips and turned, her red robe billowing around her, and headed to her taxi.

"Loeeza?" called Grodmila from inside.

Lulu stared at Cassandra's back. What did that mean? Had Cassandra known her mother or hadn't she? But then Lulu shrugged. Cassandra was right after all — her mum *was* special. And that was what mattered!

Orange Goop

Back in the kitchen, Grodmila was serving up a plate of steaming boiled cabbage. Lulu looked at it. "I'm . . . not really hungry just now, thanks." Grodmila rolled her eyes, took the plate for herself, and went off to eat it in front of the TV.

Lulu munched hungrily on Cassandra's bread as she ripped open the tiny package. Inside was a small bottle of stuff that looked like liquid sky. She dabbed some on a cloth — it smelled like crisp autumn mornings — and got to work on a candlestick. All it took was one touch, and the grunge just melted away. It was as if the grimy skin of tarnish that had enveloped the candlestick was now shriveling away, like the horns of a startled snail. Lulu was left holding a fantastically shiny piece of silver, glittering even in the nooks and crannies. She punched the air triumphantly. "Yesss!" By the time Grodmila returned, the entire pile was gleaming like new.

Crash! Grodmila dropped her tray. "Vot? Ven? How?"

Lulu smiled at her sweetly. "I just . . . worked really hard!"

As soon as Grodmila disappeared with the vacuum cleaner, Lulu eagerly unpacked her bag of goodies again. She checked the time; she still had three hours left before Varaminta and Torquil returned. She took an apple from the fruit bowl, rubbed it on her T-shirt, and was about to take a bite when she remembered the stars. She took out a knife and cut the apple in half, just as Ambrosia May's book instructed. Two perfect five-pointed seed stars nestled in the glistening white flesh. How wonderfully reliable of apples, Lulu thought, that they should always have these stars inside them. Munching on the apple, she turned the oven on and fetched a bowl and a wooden spoon. Then she opened *The Apple Star* and consulted the recipe.

Pour 1 cup boiling water over the saffron and the Reasons and leave to cool.*

For the first time, Lulu noticed the asterisk at the end of this line. She read the footnote:

*1. Remember, Reasons may be used ONLY ONCE. If the recipe is repeated with the same Reasons, the liar will tell more truths than you wish them to — the truths that you hold in your head.

Lulu gulped hard and read the lines over again to be sure she had understood correctly. "The truths that you hold in your head" . . . that could be disastrous! Her greatest secret, the recipe book itself, would be discovered. So this was her only chance to get the Truth Cookie recipe right. One chance to save Dad, and her pictures, and to bring Aileen back: to restore her life to the way it should be. She finished her apple and took a deep breath. Time to begin.

She put the kettle on to boil and found the measuring cup. As she poured the hot water over the saffron and her reasons, she watched "Torquil" and "Varaminta" dissolve, turning the water orange. It was very satisfying. Now to the next part:

Combine the Asha Vahishta nuts, sun beans, sunflower seeds, and petals in a large bowl.

Lulu poured everything in and stirred.

Break the crow's eggs into a small bowl.

Gingerly, she picked up the first of the six tiny eggs. She hit the side of the bowl with it, and the shell shattered into tiny pieces. "Oh, crikey!" she sighed. As she picked the pieces out of the bowl, she saw that her hands were shaking. Calm down, she told herself. Then she had an idea. She dropped the whole lot into the bowl and smashed them. Then she got a strainer and strained them into another bowl. Perfect! On to the next step.

Add the softened camel's butter and the Idzumo honey to the eggs. Stir. Strain the Reasons and throw the paper away. Add the remaining liquid to the egg mixture.

Lulu did this and watched as everything turned a lovely deep orange color.

> Add the wet ingredients to the dry ingredients,
> and stand back.

Why "stand back"? Lulu wondered. She tipped the orange goop into the large bowl with the nuts, beans, seeds, and petals. Immediately, the mixture started to fizzle explosively, so much so that Lulu actually had to *jump* back out of the way. The fizzling grew more volatile still, and strands of golden light began to stream out of the bowl, like sunbeams. Lulu squinted. She thought she heard babbling voices as it continued to fizzle. Then gradually the sunbeams and the babbling-fizzling began to die down. Cautiously Lulu approached the bowl and peered inside. All of a sudden, one huge final bubble popped, and out of it shot a ball of sizzling hot light, right in Lulu's face. She squealed and jerked backward, clamping her hands to her face. It felt very warm. She consulted the recipe again.

> Caution: Do not approach the bowl until after
> the huge, final bubble has been expelled!

Well, thanks for that, thought Lulu. She really should have read the whole thing properly beforehand.

See footnote for an extra step that may be added at this point.

Lulu looked again at the bottom of the page and read footnote number two. She took hold of the ostrich feather as Ambrosia May instructed and waved it over the bowl. She began to recite the given words, inserting the names as the recipe instructed:

My name is **Lulu** and I wish . . .

She stifled a giggle; she felt quite absurd. She began again:

My name is **Lulu** and I wish
That **Torquil** finds this food delish
And **Varaminta** loves it too
Then speaks only words correct and true!

It was at this moment that Grodmila walked in.

Peachface

Lulu looked at Grodmila and blushed. "Um . . ." They stared at each other. Then Lulu gave a flourish with her ostrich feather, saying, "Hubble, bubble, ha-ha — I'm being a witch!"

Grodmila just gazed at her, looking worried.

"I mean, I'm practicing," Lulu added hastily. "Acting, you know, for a play."

"Oh. I see. Play. Okay." Grodmila still looked worried. "You face . . . ," she ventured.

"What about my face?" Lulu went to look in the mirror. There, centered on her nose, was a large circle of what could only be described as sunburn. Her face was every shade of pink and red, like a ripe peach. *Oops!* This would take some explaining. . . .

She waved her arms around. "Went outside . . . sun . . . no sunblock. Silly me." Then she pointed to the bowl. "Cookies for Dad and Varaminta. Surprise!"

Grodmila grinned broadly and nodded. "Ah! Good."

"Don't tell . . . sshhh!" said Lulu, gesticulating for all she was worth. At least she didn't have to worry about Grodmila seeing the recipe book, since she wouldn't understand a word of it, anyway. As Grodmila retreated to the laundry room, Lulu was filled with alarm that she might have spoiled the "magic words" by pretending she was only playing a game. She hurriedly shook the ostrich feather over the bowl, whispering: "I didn't mean the bit about me being a witch or it being a play. So, uh, forget about that part. I mean, I don't know if it makes any difference, but . . . uh, the end!"

Then, following the last of the instructions, she dolloped spoonfuls of the cookie mixture onto two baking trays. It was lovely, fudgy, gooey stuff the color of pumpkins. Lulu put the trays in the oven. As the Truth Cookies baked, the kitchen began to fill up with a fantastic buttery, nutty smell. It reminded Lulu so much of Mum, she suddenly felt like crying.

The instant Lulu had finished, Grodmila set about cleaning the kitchen. Lulu guarded her precious cookies as they cooled. *Tsshht! Tsshht!* went the kitchen spray, a whirlwind of bleach killing every trace of cookie mix in its path. Lulu knew she ought to be grateful, but she couldn't help despising Grodmila for her fondness for bleach and over-cooked cabbage and, above all, for not being Aileen.

As soon as the cookies were cool enough, Lulu put them into a plastic bag and put the bag into an airtight container lined with paper towels, protecting them — like fragile china — from the Grodmila tornado. Before disappearing upstairs, Lulu yelled above the din, "Remember: Don't tell, okay? Surprise!"

She wanted desperately to taste one, of course; it was almost unbearably tempting. But the Truth Cookie magic might make her blurt out everything about *The Apple Star* and Cassandra, even the cook-ies themselves. Then all would be lost. So instead she opened her closet and shoved the cookies safely to the back, next to the violet satin dress and match-ing shoes she was supposed to wear at Dad and Varaminta's wedding. Lulu felt a sudden pang of remorse. Poor Dad, his big day. And here she was, planning to ruin it. But how much would be ruined for him, forever, if he did marry that bloodsucker! For herself, too, for that matter — and Aileen. Oh, how she missed Aileen. No, she was doing the right thing; she was rescuing them all.

★ ★ ★

Slam! Lulu woke with a start. The front door: Torquil, Varaminta, and the doglet were back. A little thrill ran through her as she remembered the polishing, and she rushed downstairs; this was too good to miss. She made it to the kitchen just in time to see Varaminta's face with its jaw hanging.

"This . . . you . . . she . . . Grodmila, you must have helped her!"

Grodmila swore faithfully that she had done no such thing, and the third time Varaminta accused her she sniffed, kicked off her slippers, and pulled on her shoes. "I hev to go home now," she snapped. "Good-bye!"

Torquil came into the kitchen as Grodmila stormed out. As soon as he saw Lulu's face, he guffawed, "What happened to you? Ha-ha!"

164

Lulu felt her face turn even redder as she remembered her "sunburn." "I . . . went out in the garden for a while. . . ."

"What'dja do, barbecue yourself, ha! Poodle's a hot dog, Poodle's a hot dog!" Torquil chanted.

"Get lost, Torquil," Lulu retorted. "By the way, is that a zit on your face, or are you growing another nose?"

Now it was Torquil's turn to be embarrassed. He scowled and hid his nose by pretending to scratch his forehead. Varaminta was inspecting her sparkling valuables. Finally, she turned and narrowed her eyes at Lulu. "You've been up to something. I'm not sure quite what, but" — there was that penetrating stare again — "I know you, you scheming little minx!"

"I did all your polishing!" Lulu remarked indignantly. She watched as Varaminta picked up a shiny copper pot from the gleaming pile on the counter. You'd never even use those, anyway, Lulu wanted to say. It's all for show, just like the cookbooks you never read, she thought, noting that Varaminta had recently shoved Lulu's few battered old family cookbooks to the end of a shelf nearby, to make room for her own impressive array of glossy books full of fancy recipes.

The recipe books!

Lulu was suddenly filled with icy dread, for there, innocently tidied away by Grodmila, on the shelf between those untouched volumes, sat her little golden book, *The Apple Star*. How *could* she have forgotten to put it away?

"What are you staring at?" demanded Varaminta suspiciously.

"Me? Uh . . . oh, nothing! I mean . . ." Lulu gulped. Her hands felt clammy. Varaminta turned to see what Lulu was looking at.

"Your . . . hair looks particularly nice today!" Lulu ventured, trying not to sound desperate.

"What?" spat Varaminta.

"No, really," insisted Lulu, getting carried away now. "I just couldn't help noticing how much like a precious metal your hair is . . . we've been learning about it at school . . ."

"You've been learning about my hair?"

"No, about metals, and how they —"

Lulu didn't finish her sentence, for at that

moment the phone rang. She couldn't contain her relief. "That's Dad!" she almost shrieked, deliberately staying rooted to the spot so that Varaminta would pick up first and not have a chance to discover *The Apple Star*. Poochie bounced over to the phone like a furry pink spaceball, followed by Varaminta.

"Hello? Mikey dahling! Everything's under control. Waxia's been simply mah-velous. Did you get my necklace? Well yes, diamonds for the wedding, of course . . . you got them? Wonderful! But don't forget I need something for Monday as well . . . the registry office . . ."

Lulu raced upstairs to the other phone. "Dad?"

"Hello, my love."

"Oh, Lulu darling. Do you mind, I have —"

"I've only got a moment," said Dad. "I'm just heading out. Just wanted to say I can't wait to see you both tomorrow. I'll be there in the morning!"

"Dad, what's happening at the —" began Lulu.

There was a loud crackle on the line, then Dad said, "Can't wait to see you, Noodle!"

"Dad, what was Varaminta saying about the registry off —"

"Mikey DAH-LING!" Varaminta interrupted. "About the jewelry . . ."

"Don't worry, Minty," Dad sounded tired. "I'll find something. Work's been very busy. . . ."

"Don't forget the summer fair!" Torquil called out behind Varaminta.

"Oh yes. Michael sweetie? There's this thing at Torquil's school tomorrow. I'm sure it'll be frightful, but Torquil's the star of the talent show with his karate, so naturally we have to be there. It's at three o'clock."

"Oh, that should be okay," said Dad. "I can sleep in the morning."

"Now, Mikey darling, tell me more about the diamonds. . . . What kind of necklace did you get?"

Lulu gave up. At least she'd been saved by the telephone, but her precious recipe book was still sitting there on the shelf for all to see. It wasn't until midnight that Lulu had a chance to retrieve it, and for once, it all went smoothly. Finally it was back in its hiding place and Lulu could relax. She jumped into bed and hugged her knees. "Mum, I did it!" she whispered to Grainy-Christmas-Mum. The wedding was next weekend; she had six days left. Six days in which to get Varaminta and Torquil to eat the cookies and reveal their true selves. Then all the lives they were messing up would run smoothly again. But something was still niggling at the back of her mind: the registry office. Wasn't that a place for getting married, if you weren't having a church wedding? But it was a church wedding; St. Luke's, next Saturday. *Chow!* magazine and everything. Lulu frowned in the darkness, puzzled. Oh well, she shrugged. Perhaps there's something else happening at the registry office. And before long, exhausted, she fell into a deep sleep.

St. Toast's

Lulu stood outside the church, waiting, clutching the bag of cookies. She'd gotten there first, which was important; but where was everyone else? The street was deserted. She ran to the end of the street; they had to be around here somewhere! She must find them quickly; time was running out. She checked the bag. The label said:

> Le Bone Lunch
> Eat in 5 mins

Three minutes had already passed; another two, and all would be lost. She peered around the corner: still no sign of them. She looked at the bag again; the orange cookies were turning blue with mold at the edges. Oh, help! At that moment a black taxi rounded the corner and came toward her. Finally! Here they come. . . .

The taxi pulled over alongside her and came to a stop, engine still running. Lulu's heart was aflutter as she waited for them to emerge. The taxi just stood there rattling, rattling; she peered through the windows, but they were dark. She pulled on the handle, but it wouldn't open; she looked at the cookies and now they were more blue than orange. And maddeningly, tauntingly, the taxi went *rattle rattle rattle . . .*

★ ★ ★

Clunk! Lulu heard the front door and opened her eyes.

"Hello-o, I'm ho-ome!"

Dad! Lulu leaped out of bed, her heart still pounding from the dream. Thank goodness it was just a dream! She heard the taxi roll away outside. "Dad!"

Varaminta was already in the kitchen in her long cream silk robe, one kitten-heeled slipper raised behind her as she clung to Dad like superglue.

"Mhmf!" said Dad, eyebrow raising at the sight of Lulu. He extended his one available little finger and did his best to work himself free of the Varaminta web of glue. Varaminta pouted.

"Noodle! Come here," said Dad, pulling her into

a hug. Lulu felt the prickles of his unshaven cheek against her own burnt one. "Hey, what happened to your face?"

"Nothing. Er, I'm just . . . partly embarrassed!"

Dad gave a half-laugh, clearly unconvinced. But he had other things on his mind. "Just you wait till you see what I got for your birthday!" He pulled out a little velvet box from a shopping bag.

Lulu opened the box; inside was a silver necklace with a star-shaped pendant. Lulu let out a little gasp of surprise. "Oh, I love it!" she cried.

"Glad you like it," said Dad. "You might want to wear it at the wedding!"

Lulu felt another stab of guilt. But as she watched Varaminta tearing at her own packages like a hyena, Lulu suddenly remembered something.

"Dad?" she said, when Varaminta had finished slathering over him for a second time.

"Yes, love?"

"Is something special happening tomorrow? Varaminta said something about a — registry office?"

Dad poured himself a mug of coffee. "Oh yeah," he said casually. "We have to get officially married there first. You won't miss anything. It's very dull, just signing a form, really. Only Waxia and Leo from work are coming, as witnesses. The real ceremony's at the church."

Lulu felt a rush of panic. "But I don't understand; why do you have to get married twice?"

Dad came back to the table and sat beside her. "We're not. The church won't marry us because Varaminta's divorced; Saturday's thing is a service of blessing. . . . Are you okay?"

Varaminta broke off from gazing at herself in the mirror and glanced over suspiciously.

"Oh yes," said Lulu, who definitely wasn't okay. Tomorrow. They were getting married tomorrow.

Every time she thought she was winning, something new came along to trip her up.

Dad put his arm around her. "Oh, hey! You're not missing anything — is she, Minty?"

Varaminta eyed Lulu in the mirror. That X-ray stare. "Of course not."

Lulu shivered; there was that awful rubber band feeling again. She remembered Cassandra's words: Don't let her have this power over you, or it will rot you from the inside out. Cassandra was right — she had to fight against these silly guilty feelings.

"Dad, did you call Aileen?"

"Once or twice, but I haven't managed to get hold of her."

"It's Sunday morning," Lulu pressed. "She's probably home now; will you try again?"

Dad rubbed his eyes, which were very red. "Mmm, a little later, love."

"But, Dad, you promised. . . ."

Varaminta turned away from the mirror again. "Michael, we need to have a talk because, quite honestly, I'm worried about Louisa. I didn't want to mention it when you were away, but" — her lower lip trembled and she bent down and scooped up Poochie, rubbing her face against his pink-streaked fur — "Oh, Mikey, I've been so *hurt*!"

Lulu's jaw dropped open. Was there nothing this woman wouldn't stoop to? It was all part of her plan to eat away at Lulu from inside, like a worm in an apple. "You've been hurt?" Lulu retorted. "What about me?"

"Now, hold on, hold on, what's been going on around here?" said Dad. "Is this about the bedroom thing?"

Lulu and Varaminta both answered at the same time. "About the bedroom thing," said Lulu, "and Aileen, and cabbage, and *Chow!* and . . ." She trailed off, knowing it was hopeless.

Meanwhile Varaminta carried on. "Really, Mikey, you need to talk to Louisa about her overactive imagination. All I want is for us to be one big happy family. . . ."

Lulu thought about the cookies. We'll see who's telling the truth. Her heart beat faster; this is it, do it now! But Torquil wasn't up yet; got to have Torquil too. She considered waking him up. But just as she was trying to figure it all out, Dad stood up, scraping his chair across the floor. "I can't deal with this now," he croaked. "I've had two hours of sleep, and I'm going to bed. I'll be up in time to go to Torquil's school. Good night!"

Lulu retreated to her room. She paced up and down, each time walking over the bed that now practically filled the tiny space. Calm down, she told herself, there's still this afternoon. But they were supposed to be going to the school fair, so she would have to wait until after that, unless . . . she came to a sudden halt. That was it! Why not take the Truth Cookies to the school fair? There was bound to be a cake stand; she would pretend to have bought the cookies there. Much better than having everyone know she'd made them. It was the perfect setup.

Her stomach churned with excitement, and she started pacing and fretting again. But what if the cookies didn't work? What if she'd messed up the magic words? What if Varaminta and Torquil wouldn't eat them? She was distracted by a tap at the window; it was Frenchy, throwing pebbles. Lulu waved to her, and ran downstairs and out the side door, where Frenchy was waiting.

"Wow! What happened to your face?"

Lulu rolled her eyes and groaned. She half-closed the door behind her and whispered, "It's a long story. Hey, what are you doing here, anyway?"

Frenchy glanced over at her father, waiting

in his car with the engine running, his nose deep in a newspaper. "I've only got a minute," she said in a low voice. "I got him to swing by on the way to Mum's." She grabbed Lulu's arm. "Did you make them yet?"

Lulu huddled closer. "Yes!" she hissed. "And listen, is there any way you can get to St. Toast's this afternoon? We've got to go to their summer fair. This is my big chance, French!"

Frenchy frowned and fiddled with her glasses. "Um . . . well, I don't think we have any special plans."

"There's something else," added Lulu, her voice taking on a grave tone. "You'll never guess what; they're getting married *tomorrow*!"

"No! But how come . . ."

"I've only got this one chance," said Lulu, dramatically. "Nothing can be allowed to go wrong."

Frenchy blinked at her. "Hey, hang on! It's not as bad as all that; even if you're too late, it wouldn't be the end of the world. They could just get divorced."

"No, no, no," squeaked Lulu. "I mean one chance with the cookies; the recipe will never work again!"

"Really?" said Frenchy.

"Yes, really." Lulu looked around anxiously. "I'd better go. See what you can do, okay? I may need some help."

The Cake Stand

Around two o'clock that afternoon, Dad reappeared, refreshed and clean-shaven. By a quarter to three, they were ready to go. "What have you got in that backpack?" sneered Torquil.

"Just some books. In case I get bored," Lulu retorted.

"You silly old Noodle," said Dad. "You don't want to carry that thing around with you all afternoon. Leave it behind!"

"NO!" insisted Lulu, a little too loudly.

Dad raised his hands in a gesture of peace. "All right, all right!"

Varaminta gritted her teeth. She was pretending not to mind that Lulu was joining them.

Lulu was relieved to see that even Varaminta wouldn't wear a diamond necklace to such an event, but she still stood out like a Martian. She wore a hat like a flying saucer, with alien sunglasses to match. While everyone else wore sneakers, she struggled with high heels on the soft grass.

As soon as they got there, Torquil disappeared with some friends, and some other parents came over to talk to Dad and Varaminta. Right, thought Lulu, time for action. "I'm just going to walk around," she said.

"All right," said Dad. "We'll be around here if you need anything."

Lulu found her way to the cake stand, which was, thankfully, well away from where either Varaminta or Torquil were at that moment. At one end of the table was a large tea urn. Lulu stood beside it, positioning herself so that she couldn't be seen by the woman running the stand, a barrel-shaped mother with a loud voice who was wearing a ridiculous dress with teddy bears on it. Lulu glanced furtively around, then put her backpack on the ground and took the padded container from inside it. She removed the bag of cookies.

"Ooh, those do look delicious!" came a voice from above her head. Lulu looked up. It was the woman in the teddy-bear dress. She reached out to take them. "Thank you very much. What sort are they?"

"Oh no!" said Lulu, barely able to conceal her panic. "They're not for —"

"Come on! All for a good cause!" said the woman bossily, and snatched them from her. "Look at these, Martha," she said to her helper. "Aren't they unusual! What shall we say, two pounds for the bag?"

Lulu blinked in disbelief as her precious cookies were placed among the cakes and other goodies on display. A small crowd of people were nosing around the stand. Lulu's eyes burned as she saw a hand reach over and pick up the bag. "NO!" she cried out.

Several faces turned and stared at her. "I . . . that is, I was going to buy those!" She delved into her purse and found . . . fifty-six pence. "Oh, good grief, I'll be right back!" She dodged this way and that through wandering groups of people, her mind racing. One pound and . . . one pound and . . . "Dad!" she gasped as she reached him. "Can I have one pound and forty-four pence, please?"

Dad handed her some change. "All right, but hurry back and I'll take you to the game . . . stands." He stared after the fast-disappearing figure of Lulu, and frowned.

Lulu was panting heavily by the time she got back to the cake stand. It was very busy now, and she had to wedge herself in between customers. Her eyes widened as she stared at the table; the cookies were gone! So were the teddy-bear woman and her friend! Now an Indian woman was serving, dealing with one customer while several others waited, holding out their money.

". . . That'll be two pounds fifty, please," she said, handing the customer a package of chocolate brownies.

Lulu's eyes searched wildly. "The orange cookies!" she butted in desperately.

The woman serving shot her an irritated look. "You'll have to wait your turn; there is a line, you know!"

"I'm sorry, it's just . . . they're mine. Did the other lady put them aside for me?"

The woman took the customer's money, saying, "Thank you, and . . . here's your change." She turned back to Lulu, flustered. "Put what aside?"

"My cookies!" croaked Lulu, pointing. "They were right there, bright orange. I need to buy them back!"

"Oh, those. No, they've been sold." She turned to the next customer. "Yes, can I help you?"

"But I was coming back for them!"

"Look, I'm sorry, I didn't know. Now will you please —"

"Who bought them?" Lulu squeaked.

The woman waved a hand and sighed. "Oh, a man . . . in a white shirt. Now if you'll please . . ."

Lulu turned around to face the ever-growing crowd of fairgoers. There were simply dozens of men in white shirts.

The Cookie Crumbles

"Come along, love!" said Dad. "Let's try and win something, eh?" He steered Lulu over to the game stands. Lulu moved along as if in a trance, staring ahead and seeing nothing.

"Ev'ryone's a winner!" called out a hawker. "Try it, nothing to lose!" he went on in a most annoyingly cheery manner.

I already lost! was all Lulu could think. If only she could shake off Dad and search for the Truth Cookies. But he had swooped down on her, full of enthusiasm, and they were alone together for the first time in ages. Varaminta, already bored and irritable, was sitting in a shady spot, talking on her cell phone.

"Go on, Noodle," said Dad. "Try the ring toss. Look, you could win a chocolate-making kit."

Just to please Dad, Lulu threw the ring. But she wasn't keeping her eye on the game, and every time a man in a white shirt walked past, she swung around and ended up throwing the ring way up in the air, or into the next stall. As she bent to collect her ring from the ground for the fifth time, trying all the while not to burst into tears, she spotted Frenchy and her mum at the lottery stand. She flung the ring, which went sailing over her shoulder.

"Hey, French!" she cried, and Frenchy trotted over, while her mother bought lottery tickets.

"Hey," said Frenchy, feigning surprise. "Imagine seeing you here!"

"Yeah!" said Lulu lamely.

"Hello, Frenchy," said Dad. "What are you doing here?"

"Oh . . . my cousin's at this school," Frenchy lied. "Can I borrow Lulu for a minute?"

"You might want to give her hoop-throwing lessons while you're at it," quipped Dad. "She's all over the place, like a windmill!"

"Disaster!" Lulu announced gravely, as soon as they were out of earshot.

"What? What happened?"

"They're gone!"

Frenchy gasped. "Gone? How?"

"Never mind how; somewhere in this crowd, there's a man in a white shirt who's got them. Oh, I can't believe it. We've *got* to get them back!"

Frenchy took on a look of steely determination. "Right. Don't worry, Lu, we'll find them. What do they look like?"

"You can't miss them; they're orange, pumpkin color, and they're in a clear plastic bag. . . ." She paused as she caught sight of another man in a white shirt, then sighed when she saw he didn't have the cookies. "We've got to go and watch Torquil in a minute," she went on. "Over there, in that big tent. Catch me then."

Frenchy nodded and popped a piece of gum in her mouth, ready for her mission.

★ ★ ★

Lulu failed miserably at the fishing game, the coconut shy, and the guess-how-many-pennies-in-the-jar stand. White shirts went this way and that, radiant in the sunlight, but no sign of orange cookies and no sign of Frenchy. So much for cunning, thought Lulu. I'm hopeless.

Dad seemed to have forgotten the troubles of

that morning — or was pretending they didn't exist — and was so jolly, so thrilled to be back. "How's school? Did you finish that project? What's this new Grodmila like? How was your sleepover?" And Lulu, who was not jolly, and not thrilled, could only answer "yes," or "no," or "all right, I suppose." So Dad talked and talked about his work, and New York, and the annoying guy who kept stealing other people's ideas, especially Dad's, and pretending he'd thought of them. Lulu felt as if her brain would burst.

All too soon, Varaminta teetered over; it was time to go and watch Torquil in the tent. Inside the tent, a boy was onstage torturing a violin while a teacher with a desperate, sweaty grin accompanied him on the piano. Dad found them a table and they sat down. Lulu cast her eyes around.

Then she saw him. A large man in a white shirt was standing by a table halfway across the tent, hand on hip as he chatted to someone. Dangling from the same hand, unmistakably pumpkin-colored, were Lulu's Truth Cookies! The boy onstage finished his piece, and there was a ripple of polite applause. He took his bows and left the stage. Lulu stared bug-eyed as the man casually opened the bag and helped himself to one of the cookies.

"... And now Torquil le Bone and Liam Pringle will demonstrate some karate moves," said the announcer. "Ladies and gentlemen, Torquil le Bone and Liam Pringle." There was more applause; Varaminta removed her alien sunglasses and clapped louder than anyone else. The man in the white shirt hung his jacket over the back of a seat, put the cookies on the table, and walked off.

"I've just got to go to the bathroom," piped up Lulu, right at the moment Torquil appeared onstage.

Varaminta tossed her head in disgust. "Uughh!"

"Torquil's only on for five minutes," whispered Dad. "Wait till afterward!"

Oh, Frenchy, Frenchy, come on! thought Lulu. Torquil smirked at the audience, then turned to his opponent. Another boy stood on the left, announcing the moves. "The lunge punch and the turning head block..." Torquil aimed himself fist-first at the wispy Liam Pringle. Lulu groaned inwardly and desperately scanned the tent for Frenchy. At last, she caught sight of her and, red-faced with anxiety, tried to point with her eyes at the cookies. Frenchy looked confused. Lulu noticed that the man in the white shirt was on his way back, with two other people. Desperate, she shot her arms skyward and pretended to stretch, then pointed with her finger. Frenchy's eye followed the direction of the pointing finger. Eventually her gaze alighted on the table with the orange cookies, just as the man in the white shirt and his friends got back to it.

Lulu watched as Frenchy stood up and glanced all around her, then headed over to another man in a white shirt, one with a huge camera around his neck. What on earth was she doing? Now she was talking to him! No, no . . . had she completely mis-understood? Now she was pointing; now the man-in-white-shirt-with-camera was heading over to the table where the man-in-white-shirt-with-cookies was sitting.

There was a round of applause. "And next we have the roundhouse kick," announced the boy onstage.

Now camera man was talking to cookie man and

his friends. Now the most marvelous thing was happening: All three of them were turning their backs to the table. They were posing for a picture! And now Frenchy — clever, clever Frenchy — was sneaking around behind them and grabbing the bag of cookies.

"Aah!" sighed Lulu, slumping back in her chair. Frenchy's mum had just come into the tent; Frenchy joined her and they went to sit at a table nearby. Frenchy winked at Lulu.

"Thank you, Liam Pringle and Torquil le Bone!" More applause. Torquil took his bow, while Liam Pringle picked his delicate little frame up off the floor.

Varaminta clapped loudly, shouting, "Bravo! Bravo!"

Dad stood up. "Okay, I'll go and get us some drinks. You can go to the bathroom now, Lulu."

"Oh yeah," said Lulu. "And I'll get us some cookies!"

Fish Mouth

When Lulu returned, happily clutching the precious bag, Dad, Varaminta, and Torquil were all at the table. Perfect! And they weren't alone. As she got closer, she saw that they had been joined by their next-door neighbor, Ian Cakebread, and a little boy.

"Ah, Lulu. Look who's here," said Dad. Ian and Lulu greeted each other.

"This is Ian's nephew Simon, who's in the elementary," Dad continued, pouring her some lemonade.

"What have you got there? Ooh, those look good!"

Lulu emptied the cookies onto a paper plate. "I bought them at the cake stand. Here, try them," she said, trying not to sound too eager. She handed the plate around, passing Ian and Simon so swiftly they just managed to collect one each. Mustn't waste them, she thought. Dad and Torquil made a lunge for the plate as soon as it came near them.

"Mmm, delicious!" said Dad. "Unusual. Minty, you must try one."

Varaminta scoffed, "Mikey, really, you know I don't eat that sort of thing! Loaded with fat, *ugh!*"

Lulu was prepared for this. "Oh no," she said. "They're fat-free, actually. Go on, they're really yummy and not at all *fattening*, at all, in any way."

Varaminta grimaced. "I'm not hungry."

Oh, drat! thought Lulu. Short of cramming one in Varaminta's mouth, there was nothing more she could do. But it hardly seemed to matter: Torquil was apparently very hungry indeed. Lulu watched gleefully as he helped himself to his third cookie. It was time to put a Truth Cookie to the test!

But before Lulu could do or say anything, Mr. Spratt, the principal, stopped by to congratulate Dad and Varaminta on their forthcoming wedding.

"Wasn't Torquil marvelous!" gushed Varaminta.

"Mmm, well done, Le Bone," said Mr. Spratt.

"Yeah, I love getting Pimply Pringle," said Torquil. "He's such a mummy's boy."

There was an awkward silence. Mr. Spratt's eyebrows rose, while Varaminta's grin lowered a notch or two. She just managed a forced little laugh.

Lulu sat up, intensely interested. She thought Torquil looked a little surprised at himself.

"Ahem, would you like one of these?" said Varaminta, offering the cookies to the principal.

"Thank you," said Mr. Spratt, taking one. "Of course," he added, giving Torquil a pointed look, "at St. Toast's we try to instill a sense of *brotherliness*; I'm sure Torquil's instructor would agree that karate's not about 'getting' people."

"Ab-solutely," agreed Varaminta, frowning earnestly.

There was another awkward pause. "I enjoyed the speech you gave," said Ian Cakebread.

"Oh yes," Varaminta chipped in, simperingly. "Really super."

"Ha!" snorted Torquil. "That's baloney!"

Lulu felt her ears prick up, and everyone else looked taken aback. The cookies were working! They really were working!

Torquil turned to Mr. Spratt and pronounced loudly, "Actually, she thinks you're a boring old fart!"

Varaminta stared at Torquil, fish-mouthed.

"Torquil!" exclaimed Dad. Torquil, Lulu noticed, looked just about as shocked as everyone else.

"Well, Torquil," said Mr. Spratt coolly, as he finished off his own Truth Cookie. "However boring your mother might find me, it's nothing to how tiresome I find her. . . ."

Dad stood up. "Now, just a minute, that's my —"

". . . And as for you, Torquil," Mr. Spratt went on, ignoring him, "you're a nasty little weasel, always have been, always will be. I'll see you in my office, first thing tomorrow morning. Good day." And he walked away.

"Mikey, how dare he!" gasped Varaminta indignantly.

"Now, hang on . . ." Lulu's dad started after the principal, but Lulu grabbed him by the arm and pulled him back into his seat. "Dad, never mind that. Torquil's got something important to tell you. Go on, Torquil, tell us what really happened with those pictures of my mum."

"Oh, for heaven's sake," spat Varaminta, "this is the absolute limit!"

Ian Cakebread stood up to leave. "Well, this is all very embarrassing," he said, "and right now I'd rather be elsewhere!" He carefully avoided eye contact with anyone as he started to shuffle away, looking shocked at the situation and at himself as well.

"Oh, got to feed Sushi, do you?" asked Lulu quickly, her mind abuzz. "How is she these days? . . . Is she okay?"

Eager to get away, Ian tugged at his nephew, who was still playing with his friend. "Er, Sushi's fine, thank you. Come along, Simon. . . ."

"That's good," said Lulu loudly. "Must have been so upsetting for her to be snatched like that."

Ian Cakebread blinked at her. "I'm sorry, I don't quite . . ."

"Torquil knows what I'm talking about. Don't you, Torquil?"

There was silence. Lulu stared at Torquil. Torquil's face turned pink, then purple. His eyes bulged and his lips thinned with the effort of keeping them shut. He looked like a cartoon character who had just swallowed a grenade. Finally he scrunched his eyes shut in dismay, and the words exploded from his mouth: "Yes, it was me!" he panted. "I stole your cat. I hid her in the cellar so I could get the reward money!"

There were gasps of horror all around the table. Varaminta turned to stone.

"It's true," said Lulu. "I found the litter box he used. And the empty tuna cans."

Ian Cakebread's voice was shaky. "You did that to my Sushi? I thought she'd been run over! You evil boy!" he yelled. Lulu noticed that people at surrounding tables were beginning to turn and stare.

"Oh, blah, blah!" sneered Torquil. "It's only a stupid cat!"

Suddenly Dad leaned forward. "I've never liked you, Torquil, and now you've shown your true colors. I've always suspected you were a bully, but this takes the cake. You're a . . . a monster!" Then he fell back into his seat, staring intently at the table, apparently in shock at what had just come out of his mouth.

Varaminta's face was flaming with a mixture of rage and embarrassment. "Shhh!" she hissed, desperate not to attract attention. Hastily she put her sunglasses back on, got up, and stalked past Dad, uttering, "How dare you insult my baby!" through gritted teeth. She rushed to Torquil's side and pleaded, "Why are you telling such lies, my love?" She turned to the others. "He's ill . . . he doesn't know what he's saying!"

Lulu became aware of the man with the camera yet again, loitering nearby. This time there was a young dark-haired woman with him, carrying a big black bag. They seemed to be taking a close interest in the goings-on, and now Lulu could see that they both wore badges saying HAM-ON-RYE WEEKLY. Of course! They were the local reporters. Good. The more people who knew about this, the better.

Lulu raised her voice. "I couldn't tell you about it before, Dad. He did have my pictures of Mum. He still has all the important ones. He's been holding them for ransom so I wouldn't tell about Sushi. Isn't that right, Torquil?"

Torquil held his hands up in resignation. "It's all true," he admitted. Varaminta was clearly speechless, for once unable to twist everything to her son's advantage.

The reporters were getting closer. "Is that who I think it is?" the photographer asked his companion.

"Wow. I remember her from the eighties!"

Varaminta, hearing this, glanced around. She let out a little yelp at the sight of the reporters; this was not the sort of publicity she was after. She grabbed Torquil by the hand. "Run!" she commanded. Torquil leaped up and made a dash for it, and Varaminta hobbled along behind him.

"Don't let him get away!" yelled Ian Cakebread, "HE STOLE MY CAT . . . *AND* SEVENTY-FIVE POUNDS!"

Lulu jumped up. "There's more, Dad," she urged, grabbing him by the arm. "Come on!" And she pulled him along, followed by Ian Cakebread with Simon and the two reporters.

Varaminta and Torquil left the tent and weaved their way into the crowds. Lulu emerged from the tent and blinked in the sunlight. She couldn't see them anywhere. Then she saw Varaminta's flying-saucer hat, caught by a gust of wind, spinning UFO-like toward the ground near the cake stand.

"Over there!" she cried, and the others ran ahead. Lulu pulled on Dad's arm, but he wouldn't move.

"I'm not sure I can do this," he said, dazed.

"But, Dad, there's so much more! Please, it's really important!"

"Why don't you just tell me now and get it over with?"

"Dad, she's told you so many lies." Lulu felt her eyes fill with tears. "But you have to hear it now, over there, from him. Otherwise she'll just twist the truth around again. You watch her face and you'll know. *Please*."

Dad bit his lip, gazing into the distance. Lulu gulped. Her mouth was dry as paper.

"Dad? If nothing else, do it so we can get back those pictures of Mum. He's got my favorite cards from her, my Mum-in-Muddy-Wellies photo . . . what if he destroyed them all?"

Dad was like a kettle that had finally reached boiling point. "The little devil!" He grabbed Lulu by the hand and gave it a squeeze. "Come on, then, let's go."

Hot Dog

They got to the cake stand, but everyone had gone. Then Frenchy appeared, breathless. "They went that way!" she cried, pointing toward the bouncy castle. "Come on!"

On the way, they caught up with the newspaper people and Ian Cakebread and Simon. "They split up," the photographer was telling his colleague. "You follow the boy, I'll take the mum." The young reporter nodded and dashed off after Torquil. Dad, Ian Cakebread, and Simon joined her, while Lulu and Frenchy stayed with the photographer. They headed in the direction of the bouncy castle and finally caught sight of Varaminta, her path blocked by children waiting their turn.

"Out of my way!" she demanded impatiently, as the knot of children failed to unravel itself. She pushed a small boy, and he fell face-first into his neighbor, banging his nose.

"Hey, who do you think you are?" bellowed a huge man, blocking her way.

Varaminta looked over her shoulder and saw that her pursuers were almost upon her. She tried to dodge past the big man. "Let me through!" she screeched.

An angry mother marched up with the assaulted boy, whose nose was now bleeding profusely. "Look what you did to my son!"

There was no way out; Varaminta did the only thing she could. She jumped into the bouncy castle, still in her high heels.

"No shoes!" yelled the big man, just as Varaminta's spike heel burst into the huge yellow air bubble beneath her, and she fell backward and lost her sunglasses. She removed her shoes and flung them away. Those kids still on the bouncy castle fled for cover from the spiked missiles. The castle was rapidly deflating, and Varaminta reeled this way and that, desperately trying to get to her feet.

The photographer was happily clicking away. "Ha-ha! Fantastic!" Lulu giggled, in spite of her nerves.

Then, just as the angry mum flung herself forward to grab Varaminta's ankle, Varaminta threw herself at the back wall of the castle and launched herself over it.

Lulu, Frenchy, and the photographer wove through the growing crowd to get around the side of the shrunken castle, and now they were joined by the big man, the bleeding boy, and his mother. Varaminta, freed from her spiked heels, was making swift progress. She was rejoined by Torquil just as they reached the pony trail. Torquil, with Ian, Simon, Lulu's dad, and the reporter close behind, simply dashed across the trail instead of going around. For a moment, Varaminta flapped her arms helplessly, but then she flung herself after Torquil and instantly found herself ankle-deep in pony poop.

"*Ugghh!*" she gagged. But she was stuck, and Lulu's posse was catching up too. Despite this, Torquil stopped running and doubled up with laughter at the state of his mother. His mood had changed; no longer anxious, he seemed to be thoroughly enjoying himself. Suddenly he bounded over to the nearby barbecue stand, which was doing a brisk business selling sizzling burgers and hot dogs. A line of people was waiting to be served, while others filled the picnic tables, munching away. Finally, thought Lulu, as she breathlessly approached; perhaps now she would have the chance to ask Torquil more questions.

When she arrived, Torquil was standing on a picnic table, waving a long fork with a hot dog on the end. "Hey, you guys," he jeered. "Know what you're eating there? Slimy nostrils and pigs' bottoms! Hormones and chemicals. Ha-ha! I'm gonna make millions outta these things one day" — he bent down, jabbing the hot dog at each face in turn — "from suckers like you!"

"Tell . . . everyone . . . what your mum . . . did to me on my birthday!" Lulu gasped. The newspaper reporter moved up close to Torquil and held out her microphone.

"Oh, look, it's the Poodle!" said Torquil, jumping down from the table. "She shut you in your room, of course. Sounds like you deserved it. Said you were a loathsome, scheming brat, after you ran away from the beauty salon!"

"What?" gasped Dad. "Lulu, why did you run away?"

"Oh, Dad, Varaminta's a different person when your back's turned. But she always manages to hide it. . . ." Lulu turned back to Torquil. "Why did Aileen leave?"

Torquil shrugged casually. "Mum kicked her out. She was forbidden to contact you."

"I knew it!" Lulu squealed. She turned to Dad, tears welling up in her eyes. "See? I told you. I knew it!" She took a deep breath. "All right, Torquil, tell us how your mum and my dad met."

"Lulu, I know perfectly well how —" began Dad.

"No!" interrupted Lulu. "I'm sorry, Dad, but you don't. Torquil?"

"I dunno, that's Waxia's job. She fixed it; you'll have to ask her."

Dad turned pale.

"Hold on," said Lulu. "Are you saying it was part of Waxia's job to fix your mum up with a partner?"

"That's right — husband, preferably!" said Torquil.

"I knew it!" said Lulu, punching her hand.

"Not just any old husband, either," Torquil continued. "Had to be high profile, and the right kind of high profile. Oh, and well-off, natch. When your old man appeared in the newspaper —"

"The Sweet Nothings article!" said Lulu.

". . . Yeah, right . . . Mum wanted a celebrity, really, but she wasn't having much success with those, so she figured he'd have to do. But she figured she'd get him slimmed down and persuade him to fix the house up. So at least he might seem more like a celeb, even if he wasn't really one, exactly. Then she'd convince him he wanted to marry —" The last part of Torquil's sentence came out as "mffmmffmf!" as Varaminta lunged forward and clapped a hand over his mouth.

"It's your daughter who's evil!" she screeched at Dad, wild-haired and with her bare feet covered in mud and manure. "She's got him hypnotized, or something! She —"

It was at precisely this moment that a huge hot dog, nestled in a soft bun and lavishly drizzled with ketchup and mustard, was raised aloft by a disgusted barbecue server and wedged squarely into the mouth of Varaminta le Bone.

Click! went the photographer's camera.

Nut Case

EX-MODEL GOES ON CRAZED RAMPAGE AT SCHOOL FETE

SON ACCUSED OF FRAUD

REPORT BY TRISHA DISHDURTT

Visitors to the annual summer fair at St. Toast's School for Boys were stunned when their peaceful afternoon was interrupted by a cops-and-robbers-style chase.

Ian Cakebread, of Mill Lane, crashed through the crowds with his band of vigilantes, in pursuit of Torquil le Bone, 13 years old, also of Mill Lane and a pupil at the school. Young Le Bone tricked Mr. Cakebread into rewarding him £75 for finding his valuable Siamese cat. The cat, thought to be lost at the time, is now alleged to have been stolen and hidden by Torquil instead.

But it was Torquil le Bone's mother who made the biggest spectacle. Faded star of the catwalk, Varaminta le Bone, who wouldn't tell us her age, fought like a wildcat as she tried to get herself and her son away from the scene. "She went bonkers," said an onlooker. "She ruined the bouncy castle," said another. "She assaulted my son! The nut case!" The *Ham-on-Rye Weekly* has learned that Ms. le Bone may also be guilty of cruelty to her 13-year-old future stepdaughter. Ms. le Bone is a former fashion model who is currently appearing in advertisements for Sweet Nothings no-fat cakes. She is also the author of a diet book, *How to Be as Thin as Me*.

Her agent refused to comment.

PLEA FOR RECIPE

A man in a white shirt who was present at the St. Toast's school fair has sent out a plea for the recipe of some unusual orange-colored cookies he bought at the fete. "I'd only tried one, before they were stolen from my table," he said. "It was delicious! I must have that recipe for my cookie company! We sell completely artificial cookies and cakes that we pretend are made by cute little grannies in rose-covered cottages."

Whoever baked these cookies is asked to contact Manin Whiteshirt, Cute Granny Cakes, Unit 24 Filthy Industrial Estate, London N16 5DN. The man in the white shirt also wanted it to be known that he likes nothing better than to dress up as a stationmaster and play with his train set.

★ ★ ★

There was an eerie quietness around the house on Monday. Varaminta was everywhere and nowhere. Reminders of her decorating, like the Venetian chandelier, the silk rugs, even the twenty-year-old fashion photographs, remained, although these were now stacked in a corner, facing the wall. But she, along with her precious Poochie, was gone from their lives for good. Torquil was gone for good. Getting home from school, Lulu was filled with a mixture of emotions that she found hard to unravel. After bringing her home, Dad had dropped the car keys on the hall table and gone straight upstairs, saying he'd be down in a minute. That had been half an hour ago.

Lulu jumped as the phone rang beside her. She stared at it for a moment, then picked it up.

"Lu?" said Frenchy's voice.

"French! Where were you today?"

"I got a stomach bug. I think I must have had a bad hot dog at the fair. But I've been dying to talk to you all day. What about those cookies, eh? Result, or what?"

Lulu sighed heavily. "Yeah. Result," she said lamely.

208

"Oh, I'm sorry, Lu, has it been really grim there?"

Lulu felt the tears well up. "Oh, French," she cried. "I feel so bad for my dad!"

"Has he dumped Varaminta, then?"

"Yes, and he's really upset. They were going to get married today, and now" — a sob escaped her — "now it's all over."

"But, Lu, that's fantastic, isn't it?"

"I know, I know," said Lulu, reaching for a tissue. "But I never wanted to hurt Dad." She blew her nose loudly.

"Hey, listen!" demanded Frenchy sternly. "*You're* not the one who's hurt him — *Varaminta* is! I mean, of course he's upset now that he knows how horrible she really is, but good grief, he should be down on his knees and begging your forgiveness!"

"Oh, he is!" said Lulu. "Well, not literally. But, yeah, I guess he's upset for me as much as anything else. He says he feels stupid for being taken in by her, and for not believing me about Torquil taking the Wodge of Stuff, and for going off to work and leaving me with her, and about Aileen getting fired . . ."

Lulu sniffed and took a deep breath. "But you're right. I am NOT to blame. Of course you're right."

"I know I'm right," said Frenchy.

The doorbell rang. "I'd better answer that," said Lulu. "Dad told me he didn't want to see anybody."

"Listen, everything's going to be fine, okay?" said Frenchy. "And good job! You did it, Lu!"

"Thanks," said Lulu. "And thanks for your help. 'Bye!" Lulu hung up quickly and went to answer the door. And there, on the doorstep, was Aileen.

Lulu threw her arms around her. "Aileen! You're here . . . you're actually here!"

"Oh, it's swell to see you, Lu!" said Aileen, giving her a squeeze. "How the heck are you?"

Lulu found herself bursting into tears all over again. Aileen led her back into the kitchen. "Come on, kiddo, let's have a cup of tea and a chat. Boy, I need filling in! There I was, I just got home, and there was this message on the answering machine from your dad's office: Wedding's canceled, car coming to pick me up at 3:30. That's it, *boom*. I was gobsmacked!"

Lulu peered curiously at Aileen. "You got a message from dad's office? Today?"

"That's right," said Aileen, filling up the kettle.

"Hmm, weird," said Lulu. "Dad hasn't been at work all day."

Aileen paused, the tea tin in her hands. "Well, she said she was calling on your dad's behalf. Might've been a temp, I guess, deeper voice than his usual secretary." She put down the tin and slapped her forehead. "Oh, wow, I hope this isn't some awful prank?"

Lulu shook her head vigorously. "No, no, it's all true. It's just . . . deep voice, huh?" She thought for a moment. Dad was far too preoccupied right now to have arranged this. But there was someone else who just might have something to do with it. . . . "You said a car brought you here. Was it . . . a black cab?"

"Ye-eah," said Aileen slowly, frowning.

"So did you, uh, have a nice taxi ride?" Lulu asked.

"Boy, girl, you wanna know about my *cab ride?* You Poms, I never will figure you out! This some sort of stiff upper lip thing, or what?" Aileen put her hands on her hips. "Since you mention it, yes, it was a nice ride — if a bit *unusual.* Never got a peep out of the driver — couldn't see him, actually, 'cause there were tinted windows and the curtain was drawn. But it was a comfortable ride, lovely blue velvet seats —"

"Cassandra!" Lulu whispered, in spite of herself.

"Who?"

"Oh, nothing —"

Aileen leaned on the counter. "Lulu, willya tell me what the flippin' heck is going on!"

"Hang on, I think *you've* got a bit of explaining to do too!" said Lulu, quickly changing the subject. "What was the big idea, disappearing off the face of the earth like that? I called you so many times, kept leaving you messages. What happened to you?"

"Oh, Lulu, I'm so sorry," said Aileen, reaching out and squeezing Lulu's shoulder. "I wanted to call you back so badly. It was difficult for me too, kiddo. But I didn't want to make things even harder for you. I thought you stood a better chance of getting along with Varaminta without me rocking the boat. In fact, she said exactly the same thing, right before she fired me. Wait a minute, you didn't think I just walked out, did you . . . ?"

"No, of course not. I knew you wouldn't," said Lulu, "although that's what Varaminta said. It's just that I was worried about you; I wanted so badly to talk to you."

"There's something else," said Aileen. "I needed references. You know that psychology course I wanted to take? Well, the college needed a reference before I could enroll, and I desperately needed another job too. With your dad away, Varaminta was going to do the references instead. And she said she'd give me a glowing report . . . just as long as I made no attempt to contact you."

"Oh boy, you poor thing!" said Lulu.

"So you see, I really couldn't have called. I'm sorry you've been put through all this, though, Lu. Boy, what exactly has been going on, anyhow?"

"I'll tell you everything . . . but wait a minute — did you ever get your references?"

"Nope. Nothing."

Lulu's eyes brightened. "I'll tell Dad. He can write you one right away for the college, but not for the job: You won't need it. Aileen, welcome back!"

Baloney

Two Months Later . . .

A large lopsided cake nestled on a messy plate. The table was strewn with squeezed-out tubes of colored icing and candy drops. Dad put his arm around Lulu. "Not bad for a first attempt, I suppose!"

"Don't worry, Dad," said Lulu, "you'll get the hang of it!" Dad had taken time off from work for the last two weeks of the school holidays. They hadn't gone anywhere much, except for visiting some friends out of town. It had been a lovely, relaxing time. That day, Dad had got Lulu to give him some baking lessons: "cake therapy," he jokingly called it. Lulu got up to get a glass of water. Through the window above the sink, she gazed at the apple tree, which was heavy with fruit. "Better make an apple crumble next!" she remarked.

"Mmm," said Dad, as if he hadn't really heard her.

Lulu turned and saw him gazing at the cake, in a world of his own. "Dad?"

"Huh?"

214

"You're not thinking of *her*, are you?"

"Oh, sorry. Yes, I was, actually."

"Do you miss her?"

Dad sighed. "Sometimes it just comes over me in waves, and I feel really sad."

"But . . . you don't wish you were still together, do you?"

Dad frowned. "What sort of question is that?" He stared at Lulu for a moment. "Oh! You're talking about *Varaminta?*" He laughed. "No, I was thinking about Heather . . . your mum. It's because of the cake. You remember that one she made for your fifth birthday?"

"How could I forget?"

"Boy, did she make a mess putting that together!" laughed Dad. "She never was much for cleaning up. You had this sense, when she was creating, of something else taking over. I don't know what it was, but I know I liked eating the result! Maybe I should get into cooking more; it's very satisfying. I've been far too buried in my work. Poor Noodle," he added, ruffling Lulu's hair.

"Oh, it's not really your fault, Dad," said Lulu.

"After all, you did have Varaminta spending every penny faster than you could earn it."

Dad laughed. "Well, at least that won't be a problem anymore!"

"So you don't miss Varaminta, then?"

"No! I guess I was lonely, really, and I was flattered by all the attention. But once I knew the whys and wherefores . . . boy, that Waxia certainly did her homework. She'd found out where I went for lunch, which dry cleaners I used . . . you name it! And I thought it was just coincidence that Varaminta kept popping up in those places. Anyway, after the way she treated you, and Aileen, too, I could never forgive her. No, it was a lucky escape." He looked again at the cake. "What's more, now I can eat whatever I want!" He went to get a slice of cake.

"Hey, hang on, Dad," said Lulu. "We've got to wait for Aileen; she'll be here any minute!"

"Oops, you're right!" laughed Dad. He tapped his finger on the cake, thoughtfully. "You know, I still can't figure out what made Torquil come out with all those confessions like that."

It wasn't the first time Dad had raised this question, and Lulu was finding it harder and harder to distract him when it came up. She busied herself putting away the butter, the eggs, the flour, the sugar. Yellow and white. She couldn't help smiling to herself at their ordinariness.

"What's the secret smile for?" asked Dad. "Is there something you haven't told me?"

Lulu blushed, a real giveaway. He was on to her; she'd have to say something. "Dad, I have a confession of my own to make," she said. "That day, when I ran away?"

"Yes?"

"I, uh . . ."

This book has come to you because it was meant for you, and no one else.

"That is, I . . ."

No one else . . . and she'd already shown Frenchy. She just couldn't risk telling anyone else. What if she jeopardized the magic in some way?

". . . Well, I . . . never paid the bus fare!"

★ ★ ★

Lulu took the Mum-in-Muddy-Wellies picture from the Wodge of Stuff. All the pieces were back together again, including the most important ones: the glitter monster, the birthday cake picture, the card. One of these days, she thought, I'll organize everything properly into a nice big album. She'd been telling herself this for a very long time but still hadn't gotten around to doing it. For now, Mum's assorted bits and pieces were still in the tin and held together by a new green rubber band that reminded Lulu of the bad feeling she used to get from Varaminta, that hard knot in her belly, like a big ball of rubber bands. The knot had long since melted away, and it was hard to believe she had ever allowed someone to make her feel such pain and guilt. Looking back now, Lulu realized that the feeling had not been new. She'd always felt it a little, since she was five years old and her mum went out the door and never came back to her. Varaminta had just made it worse, sniffing it out like a tiger smells fear in its prey.

Yet in a way, Lulu knew now, Mum had never really left at all. "Hey, Mum, our star is shining tonight!" said Lulu. She knelt on the bed and gazed out the skylight. Her new bedroom at the top of the house gave her a splendid view of the night sky. Over the weeks her star, the one she had found on the way to Cassandra's, had moved farther to the center of her view, along with its two little companions. She couldn't always make out the companions, or indeed the Milky Way itself, but she always knew her star: the one she called her Truth Star. Whenever she studied it, it was like focusing a lens. Things became clearer, easier to understand.

Venus was over to the right, showing off its brilliance at night, long before any of the other stars appeared. Lulu liked to think of it by its other name, Hesperus, and to imagine it shining above the beautiful garden with the nymphs and the golden apple tree.

What a load of old baloney! her old self might have said. Like believing in fairies. And of course she didn't really believe there was such a place. Of course not. But now she understood that all stories, however fantastic, had some truth in them.

The End

DATE DUE

FE 10 '06	OC 22 '07	APR 17 '09
FE 27 '06	NO 08 '07	SEP 25 '09
AP 28 '06	FEB 19 '08	OCT 07 '09
OC 11 '06	MAR 04 '08	JAN 19 '10
NO 16 '06	MAR 11 '08	MAR 15 '10
DE 13 '06	MAR 25 '08	OCT 31 '11
JA 12 '07	MAR 27 '08	JAN 17 '12
FE 14 '07	APR 11 '08	
MR 15 '07	APR 28 '08	
MY 09 '07	OCT 06 '08	
OC 01 '07	OCT 20 '08	
OC 08 '07	FEB 23 '09	